LOVE AT FIRST SIGHT

How could anyone not fall in love with Cameron? Handsome, rich, funny, caring — the sort of man every girl dreams of. And he had fallen in love with Megan. She couldn't say 'no' to his offer of marriage and she was swept along in a whirl of preparations. Was he just too good to be true? How well did she really know him? What was the old saying — 'marry in haste, repent at leisure'? She just hoped the second part wasn't true . . .

CHRISSIE LOVEDAY

LOVE AT FIRST SIGHT

Complete and Unabridged

LINFORD
Leicester

First published in Great Britain in 2008

First Linford Edition
published 2009

British Library CIP Data

Loveday, Chrissie
  Love at first sight.—Large print ed.—
Linford romance library
  1. Love stories
  2. Large type books
  I. Title
  823.9′2 [F]

ISBN 978–1–84782–564–3

Published by
F. A. Thorpe (Publishing)
Anstey, Leicestershire

Set by Words & Graphics Ltd.
Anstey, Leicestershire
Printed and bound in Great Britain by
T. J. International Ltd., Padstow, Cornwall

This book is printed on acid-free paper

Visit the author's website at:
www.chrissieloveday.com

An Eligible Bachelor

Megan shopped on her way home from work. Her best friend, Lisa, had said she didn't eat properly and she was right. All the same, a ready-made meal was so much easier than cooking from scratch, and so — planning a quiet evening at home on her own watching television, accompanied by a microwave dinner for one — she put a frozen lasagne and a pack of ready-washed leaves into her basket.

What a solitary existence I lead, she thought, and how different from the exciting life her parents thought she was living.

Once she got home, she ate the uninspiring meal and curled up on her rather uncomfortable sofa.

The phone rang.

'Hallo, darling,' said her mother. 'How are you?'

'Hi, Mum. You and Dad both well?'

'We're fine. Although, I am a little worried that your father's been overdoing it at work again.'

Her mother's voice did sound a little strained, thought Megan, and warning bells rang in her head. Her father always worked too hard but if her mother was mentioning it, then she really must be worried.

'It's simply ages since you came home.'

'I know, Mum. And I'm sorry. I just seem to get caught up in things and the weeks fly by. But I'll come home soon, I promise.'

'How about this weekend, if you're free?'

Megan's brain raced through a series of possible excuses. It wasn't that she didn't love her parents dearly, but weekends at home were always the same. A cosy dinner or drinks party, masterminded especially for her to meet the latest unattached male who her mum thought might be suitable

2

husband material.

'Well, OK — I could come up on Friday night.'

'Oh, good. I am pleased. Ewan will be at home as well. We can have a really good family weekend together.'

'Great. It's ages since I saw him.'

Although they'd fought and squabbled as children, Megan and her brother, Ewan, had become firm friends now that they were both adults, even though they saw little of each other. Ewan had just finished his final year at university and was now deciding what to do with the rest of his life.

'We've invited some of Dad's business contacts for a meal on Saturday evening, so make sure you bring something suitable to wear. Smart, I mean. Not your usual scruffy jeans.'

When they eventually said goodnight to each other, Megan gave a small sigh as she put down the phone, wishing her mother would stop trying to matchmake.

On the other hand, what plans did

she really have for the weekend? A trip to the launderette? Shopping? She was supposed to be a trendy young woman living in London, with a career in journalism that she loved. The reality was that she was stuck in a rut. She must do something about her personal life, she decided. She couldn't carry on like this, just living to work.

* * *

'It's lovely to see you,' she told her mother as she swept into her family home that Friday evening.

'You should come home more often then, darling. We're hardly at the other end of the universe. How long does it take? Forty minutes on the train, or something like that?'

Megan's mother propelled her into the lounge where her father and brother were standing next to the open window, each with a wine glass in his hand.

'Hello, you two,' Megan said brightly. 'And how are my two favourite men?'

4

They all hugged each other. 'You're both looking very serious.'

'Dad was suggesting I might like to come into the business. Take some of the load off his shoulders,' Ewan said, once they were all sitting down.

'I assumed that was taken for granted. You have all the right qualifications and Dad needs to slow down. This has to be the ideal solution all round. Besides, you're well on the way to having a gap life, let alone a gap year.'

'There you are. I said Megan would see it like that,' Mona Belmore said, smiling at her husband.

Megan's mother was still a beautiful woman with a natural grace and charm. Her hair was always immaculate, the copper colour now flecked with grey, but her green eyes, so like her daughter's, danced with the joy of a happy life. She was excited to have her both her children home.

'Dad wondered if you might feel a little jealous, Megan, if Ewan came back here to live and work,' she said now.

'For heaven's sake! I mean to say, can you ever imagine me running a shop? It would be utter chaos in five minutes flat.'

They all laughed with relief, and Megan felt the warmth of her family settling round her like a well-loved security blanket.

But 'running a shop' somewhat understated how her father made his living. Over the years he'd built up a successful chain of independent local stores that were holding their own against the relentless march of supermarkets by stocking quality, locally produced goods and giving personal service. Ewan's involvement in the company was a great idea.

★ ★ ★

'So what's happening this weekend?' Megan said later, after they'd eaten a delicious meal.

'Well, as I've already told you, we're having a few people round for dinner tomorrow night. Business chums of your father's. There will be one or two younger people so it shouldn't be too boring for you.'

'And one of them just happens to be an eligible bachelor, I suppose. You never change, do you, Mum?'

'Oh, but I do. I've quite given up on you, my dear,' Mona said with a smile.

'I see. Now it's my turn is it?' Ewan joked.

The rest of the evening passed in a light-hearted mood but Megan couldn't help but notice that her father did look very tired and strained. She'd try to find a moment during the weekend for a private chat with him, just to reassure herself that all was well.

At eleven o'clock, her parents went to bed, leaving brother and sister to talk.

'Dad doesn't look very well, does he?' Megan commented.

'I think there have been a few problems with the business. But you know what he's like. Refuses to slow down. Always trying something new.'

'Hmm. Well, I'm off to bed. I need some beauty sleep. Oh, drat! I meant to ask Mum for her hairdresser's phone number. I thought I might get my untidy mop trimmed tomorrow if she could fit me in. It's reached the uncontrollable stage again.'

* * *

As a favour, Mona's hairdresser agreed to fit in an appointment for Megan, late on Saturday afternoon.

'Your hair's not quite like your mother's, is it?' the hairdresser commented. 'It's a gorgeous colour, though What did you have in mind?'

'Well, Mum's having a dinner party tonight so I feel I need to make an effort. I don't want to do anything too drastic, though. Just a trim, but could you straighten it for me? Just for a change?'

'Are you sure? Most women would

love natural curls like yours.'

'They'd soon change their minds if they had to get a brush through it in the mornings! Let's get busy with the straighteners.'

By the time she returned home, Megan's mad curls had been temporarily transformed into straight, shiny, swishy hair, and she felt elegant and stylish.

'Who's coming this evening?' she asked as she helped her mother to lay the table.

'The Hardys and their son and daughter, and another couple. The chap's something to do with wine. He's going to supply our shops, I gather. Marshall's their name. Cameron and Jane Marshall.'

'Oh, no. Wine bores. I suppose we shall get a non-stop lecture on which side of the valley the grapes come from. Where do they live?'

'I'm not sure. Their business is somewhere over Chesham way. They do a lot of importing and direct sales. Dad met them at some do and seemed to take to them. Other than that, I know nothing about them. So, altogether, there'll be ten of us at dinner.'

'Dinner for ten? I don't know how you can ever cope with so many. I can scarcely manage a dinner for one and only then if it comes ready-made.'

'You'd manage if you had to. It just takes a bit of practice to judge quantities. I have to say,' Mona said to her daughter, 'your hair looks lovely like that, but you don't look like yourself at all. Not without the usual wild mass of tangles sprouting out of your head!'

'Gosh, thanks, Mum. That's a back-handed compliment if ever I heard one. Well, if there's nothing else I can do to help then I'm going up to change,' said Megan. 'I'll need to prepare myself to fend off the advances of the younger Hardy, not to mention his father.'

'I despair of you, Megan. Will you ever grow up and settle down?'

'And produce a brood of revolting grandchildren for you to spoil? Shouldn't think so for a minute.'

She went up to her room. The evening didn't hold much promise but she knew her parents would expect her to make an effort.

She rummaged in her wardrobe and found a pale-blue silk dress she'd forgotten she had. She tried it on and twirled in front of the mirror, noticing that she'd lost weight since she'd last worn it. The closely-fitting top hugged her body, and the neckline showed off her natural curves, perhaps slightly more than she cared for. Sitting next to either of the Hardys, the younger or the elder, could be something of a strain.

She decided to wear a less revealing, sea-green cotton dress.

She brushed her gleaming, poker-straight hair, pleased with the effect, then went down to join her family as they waited for their guests.

The Hardy family arrived first and had just been given their drinks when the doorbell rang again. Megan's parents went through to the hall to greet the Marshalls, and Megan, continuing to chat to Ewan and the others, didn't turn round to greet the newcomers until her father was doing the introductions.

'And this is my daughter, Megan. Megan, meet Cameron and Jane.'

'Pleased to meet you,' said Jane. 'It was so nice of your parents to invite us.'

The Marshalls were younger than Megan had expected. In fact, the wife looked younger even than Ewan.

'Er, yes,' burbled Megan, who was staring past Jane Marshall at her husband. He looked vaguely familiar. Very tall and with the blackest hair, he was gorgeous. Now, why couldn't her mother find a single man who looked like him to practice her matchmaking skills on?

'Hello, Megan,' said Cameron Marshall, looking at her curiously, his head slightly on one side. 'Haven't we met before?'

'I'm not sure. You do look familiar, but I can't place you.'

She had met him before, she was sure, and her mind was racing, trying to remember where, when — with slight horror — she suddenly remembered the occasion very clearly. At a press launch for a new chain of hotels, earlier in the year, she had tripped as she'd been walking past him, spilling a whole glass of red wine over his suit. An undoubtedly very expensive, pale grey suit.

Suddenly he smiled at her, his startlingly blue eyes looking straight into her own with an amused twinkle.

'At least, I thought I recognised you,' he said, much to her discomfort. 'But that girl had wild, curly hair.'

'So will Megan, tomorrow morning, once the effect of the hairdresser's straightening irons have worn off,' said Ewan, laughing.

Cameron turned to accept a drink.

'Wine's your business, I understand?' Megan asked him, desperate to deflect attention away from herself.

'Yes. I'm especially fond of French wine. Burgundy, in particular. I'd rather drink it than wear it, mind you.'

The corner of his mouth twitched as he teased her. Oh, dear. He obviously remembered her and the incident.

They sat down to dinner. Her mother had placed her between the younger Hardy male and Cameron Marshall. Jane was next to Ewan, who had Beth, the Hardys' young daughter, on his other side.

Megan was more than a little taken aback when Ewan, who seemed more than a little taken with Jane, flirted with her quite openly throughout dinner, despite her husband being seated opposite.

As for Cameron, himself, he was the perfect dinner guest, attentive and complimentary to his hosts. He talked knowledgeably about wine, but had the knack of making it sound interesting. His tales of tiny French villages and their vineyards made it sound very personal. Megan could easily believe that he knew all the vintners as friends.

'You're a newspaper journalist, so I

seem to remember?' he asked her as coffee was poured. There was still that infuriating glint of amusement in his eyes as he spoke.

'That's right. I work for one of the smaller London weeklies.'

'And do you actually work in London?'

'Mostly. Can I pass you a mint?' she asked.

★ ★ ★

The evening passed pleasantly enough, with the charming and handsome Cameron being monopolised by Mona and Mrs Hardy.

It seemed they'd both suddenly developed an interest in wines and wanted to find out everything about his business.

Around midnight, everyone took their leave, and Cameron Marshall kissed Megan lightly on the cheek as he said goodbye. He drew in his breath as if he wanted to say more, but seemed to think better of it.

Then the guests were all gone and the door closed behind them.

'Interesting woman, that Jane Marshall,' Ewan said casually.

'So I noticed,' his father replied. 'You were positively drooling.'

'I was not.'

'I wonder Cameron didn't hit you,' said Megan. 'He's obviously very tolerant, allowing you to flirt with Jane all evening.'

'Why should he hit me? I only shook hands with her in the most polite way possible. Oh! You thought they were married, didn't you? Well, they're not. They're brother and sister! Silly you! Mind you, they don't look much alike.'

Megan was speechless. Only, joy of joys! Just for once, her mother had introduced her to someone she found attractive.

'Megan,' Ewan said thoughtfully, after their parents had gone to bed, 'you'd met Cameron Marshall before, hadn't you?'

'Whatever makes you think that?' she asked, a blush creeping into her cheeks.

Her brother put a fond arm round her and gave her a hug.

'Good old Megs. Come on. What disaster did you cause?'

'I accidentally tipped a whole glass of Burgundy over his very expensive suit at a press launch. I'm still waiting for the cleaning bill.'

★ ★ ★

The rest of the weekend passed quickly for Megan. It was good to spend time with her brother again. Nowadays, he seemed more like a friend.

'It would be nice if you'd come up to London more often,' she told him. 'For such an obnoxious brat, you've turned out remarkably well.'

'Well thank you, my ancient old crone of a sister,' Ewan said with a wicked grin on his face. 'I'm seeing Jane again, incidentally. One night next week. Shall I mention the devastating effect her brother has had on you?'

'Don't you dare breathe a word. Anyway, who says I'm devastated?'

* * *

All too soon, it was Monday morning, and she was seated on the train back to London, facing another day at the office.

'Good weekend?' called Lisa as Megan headed towards her desk. 'Did your mum manage to find you a decent bloke this time?'

'Don't joke about it. You'll never believe what happened. Remember when I tripped at that press do and spilled my drink all over that guy? The drop dead gorgeous one? The one I said was the man of my dreams? Well, he was at Mum and Dad's for dinner at the weekend. It seems he's going to be supplying the family shops with wine.'

The look on Lisa's face was a picture.

'I bet you spent the entire evening flirting madly.'

'No way. He arrived with a gorgeous female on his arm. Same name. I thought she was his wife and spent the whole evening trying to be cool. Turns out she was his sister and business partner. Mum and Dad hadn't bothered to pass on such a vital detail.'

'So, any chance of you seeing him again?'

'That's just it. Because I thought he was married I played it cool. Date? Huh, some chance!'

Lisa gave her a wry grin as she went back to her own workstation.

'Megan,' called Don from the other side of the office. 'I need some information.'

She crossed to his desk.

'I'm doing a series on business success stories. Young entrepreneurs sort of thing. You might be able to help.'

He picked up a photograph and handed it to her.

She looked at it and squeaked.

Don went on, 'That's the chap I want the info about. His is one of the success stories I'm going to be writing about. He's call Cameron something or other — a wine importer. He's been buying up smaller concerns and he's now got places all over London and the Home Counties. I'm interviewing him this week and I wondered if you knew him? — He lives near where you come from. Could you give me any extra background on him? You've gone a funny colour. What's the matter?'

'Nothing. I'm just surprised at the coincidence. Cameron Marshall was a guest at a dinner party at my parents' house at the weekend.'

'Oh! Well, in that case, since you know the guy socially, maybe you could come with me to the interview on Tuesday? Break the ice, so to speak?'

She hesitated and turned a deep shade of pink. This was the perfect excuse to see Cameron again. But would it look as if she was stalking him if she suddenly turned up on his doorstep so soon after the dinner party?

Don took the photograph back. 'If

James will clear it, I'd really like to take you along, Megan. But it's my interview and I don't want you butting in. OK?'

★ ★ ★

Megan stood waiting outside the railway station on Tuesday morning. For once she was early, and had dressed and applied her make-up with extra care. She felt excited at the prospect of seeing Cameron again, and grinned as she thought how surprised he'd be when she turned up on his doorstep. She scanned the faces of the commuters passing her by, wondering where Don could be. It was most unlike him to be late. She glanced at her watch just as a car pulled up beside her and the driver leaned over to open the door.

'Want a lift, lady? Come on, dreamer,' Don said cheerfully. 'James offered me the pool car. As we're not going too far outside London, it saves the taxi hassle.'

Don chatted amiably as they drove out of town while Megan sat quietly, thinking and planning what she was going to say to Cameron when she met him again. She was beginning to feel very nervous. Much as she wanted to get to know him better, she wasn't sure this was the right way to go about it.

'There's a map in the glove compartment. Just check which turning we need,' said Don. 'I don't think we have to go into Chesham itself. He lives in some enormous great mansion out in the country, I gather. Don't know how anyone can stand all this green everywhere and so much quiet.'

Don was smiling cynically, but Megan realised he meant every word. He was a real townie.

They turned into a small single track lane and he slowed down.

'Good grief. At least in town you can see when someone's coming straight towards you.' He shook his head in disbelief. 'I hope this guy doesn't have a straw between his teeth.'

'Oh, no. Mr Cameron Marshall is very smart and sophisticated. I don't think you'll feel the least bit out of place with him.'

They turned into the driveway of a secluded house and Megan felt a shiver of excitement when she saw the large, mellow stone building.

'Wow,' Don exclaimed. 'He must be doing well with his business to be able to afford a pad like this. It must be worth millions.'

Megan was as overawed as her colleague. She felt a bit like the second Mrs de Winter driving up to Manderlay. She would not have been surprised to see Mrs Danvers standing waiting at the door, with the ghost of Rebecca behind her.

Don pulled up outside the house and smiled at his companion.

'If he's a family friend, you certainly move in different circles to me,' he said, grinning.

'Oh, but I don't.' Her nerves were jangling. She wanted to get the next few minutes over with.

But it wasn't Mrs Danvers who

opened the door but Cameron himself, looking immaculate as ever in a navy suit.

'Don Meadows,' said the reporter, holding out his hand — Cameron took it automatically, all the time staring at Megan 'And this is my associate, Megan Belmore. I understand you know each other?'

'Yes, we have met. Come in. Welcome,' Cameron said to Don. Then, 'Why didn't you tell me you were coming here?' he whispered to Megan, as they went through the hall and into the lounge.

'I didn't know until yesterday. I . . . ' she whispered back, blushing fiercely.

'I'll order some coffee,' said Cameron politely. 'Excuse me for a moment.'

He left the room and Don stared at Megan.

'Something wrong?' he asked.

'No,' she managed to squeak back. She hadn't realised just how much Cameron had affected her. Her pulse was racing and her heart pounding. She took several deep breaths, hoping to regain her self-control.

'Coffee's on its way,' said their host as he returned to the room. 'Now, perhaps you'd like to make yourselves comfortable and we can begin. I'm not exactly sure what you want to know.'

They all sat down.

While Cameron and Don chatted, Megan stared around the room.

It was furnished with exquisite taste and was beautifully proportioned. Tall windows overlooked the garden. The furniture was all antique, the mellow wood suiting the room perfectly. The soft furnishings echoed the blue and peach of the Chinese carpet.

A huge bowl of apricot-coloured roses stood on a small table in the large bay window. They could have been grown especially to fit the décor. There was something oddly extravagant about such a huge display of perfect flowers.

There were several easy chairs covered in varying shades of blue and apricot, and the pale cream walls gave a light and airy feel to the elegant room.

Cameron and Don were well into the interview, she suddenly noticed with some surprise. She must have been day-dreaming for several minutes. Most unprofessional, she chided herself. Then Jane came in with coffee.

'Megan!' she said with surprise. 'What are you doing here?'

'Hoping to chat with you,' she smiled back. 'Some background about your illustrious brother and how his rapid success is affecting your lives.'

'Oh, dear,' said Jane. 'I'm sure nothing I can say will be of interest. Now, how do you all like your coffee?'

Megan watched her, seeing at once why Ewan had been so smitten with her at first sight. She was a lovely girl, much younger than her brother. As fair as Cameron was dark, and with a gentle smile and the same, perfect white teeth as his.

She realised that she and Jane could easily become friends. If Jane and Ewan progressed in their relationship, Megan for one would be delighted.

She became aware of Cameron watching her as the coffee was passed round. When their eyes met, it was as if a link was established between them. Her heart leaped and she felt herself blushing under his scrutiny. She hated her fair complexion that allowed such blushes to give away her feelings.

The interview continued and she and Jane sat together on the other side of the room to talk.

Suddenly Jane said, 'Look, I'm not sure what your plans are but can you stay for lunch? We can talk over the meal.'

'I'm not sure what Don has planned, but it sounds lovely to me — if it isn't too much trouble.'

The two women went across to join the men.

'Jane's invited us to stay for lunch. What do you think, Don?'

'Thanks a lot. That would be great. I'm free for the day,' he replied.

★   ★   ★

Jane went off to organise the meal. Don excused himself and went to use the bathroom. Cameron took his chance.

'I wanted to ask you for a date on Saturday but you seemed a bit hostile,' he said. 'I suppose I sort of assumed you had something going with that man on the other side of you?'

'What, Alan Hardy? No fear. My parents did nurture a few hopes once upon a time but I don't see myself settled in darkest Bucks with someone like him. No — and I'd assumed Jane was your wife.'

He gave a chuckle.

'Actually, my sister was rather taken with your brother. I think they're meeting up again sometime later this week. Do you have to go back to London with your colleague? We could go out somewhere to have dinner together and then I could drive you back home.'

'I don't know what Don would think, but it sounds lovely.'

'Actually, I should confess something. I persuaded Jane to ask Ewan for your number and I tried to phone you last night, but your line was engaged for hours. I asked the operator to check in case you'd left it off the hook but she said you were talking. In the end, I decided you'd think I was being too pushy, so I gave up'

Megan felt her cheeks growing warmer.

That he should have actually gone to such lengths to see her again!

'Everything all right?' Don asked as he came back into the room, eyeing the pair with some suspicion.

'I was just asking Miss Belmore if she needed to go back to the office this afternoon,' Cameron said with not so much as a flicker.

'Well, strictly speaking, no. She doesn't have to travel back with me.'

He looked rather put out but he gave a shrug, giving Megan a look that suggested he wanted a full explanation at some time.

A Fast Mover

Lunch was a simple affair of grilled fresh salmon and salad followed by strawberries and cream. Naturally, Cameron served a wine that was the perfect accompaniment to the meal.

After lunch, the two journalists were given a tour of the house and with every room she saw, Megan loved the place more. The same good taste showed throughout and no expense had been spared to restore the lovely eighteenth century building to its former glory.

'We haven't got around to the rest of it yet,' Cameron said as they stopped halfway along a corridor. 'There are several more rooms on this floor and the whole of the upper attics to be done.'

'It's all wonderful,' Megan said with enthusiasm. 'You're doing a marvellous job. It must have cost a fortune.'

'I've been lucky. I have contacts all over the world who look out for special things for me. They know what I like. You'd be surprised at the bargains there are out there when you know the right people to ask.'

At last, Don announced it was time to drag himself away.

Megan felt uncomfortable as she saw him off. Cameron had gone back inside and Don took the chance to ask a few questions.

'He seems very keen on a certain young reporter,' Don said.

'Of course he isn't,' protested Megan.

'But you seem to know him as more than just a family friend. It's obvious.'

'I've met him a couple of times. That's all. OK?'

Don gave a shrug and drove off rather too quickly.

* * *

The rest of the day passed in a dream for Megan. She and Cameron walked through the grounds which seemed to go on for ever, talking as if they had known each other for months instead of just hours.

She felt as if she was floating on a glorious pink cloud.

Cameron explained how his parents had been killed in an accident some years before, at a time when neither he nor Jane were old enough to stand on their own feet.

Once they were of an age to decide themselves how best to use their inheritance, it had been their parents' life assurance that had provided the capital for them to establish the business and to buy the house. It was clearly a shrewd investment, and Cameron's business acumen had done the rest.

That evening, they had a meal in a cosy country restaurant, and when he took Megan home, Cameron's beautiful silver sports car ate up the miles and they arrived at her London home in much too short a time.

She dreaded asking him in as the flat was chaotic. She'd missed her cleaning session at the weekend and the place was even more untidy than usual.

'I . . . I should ask you in for coffee,' she said hesitantly. 'But I'm sure you need to get back after spending so much of the day with us. With me.'

'But I'd love a coffee,' he said smoothly. 'And don't worry about the mess.'

'How did you know . . . ?'

'Just guessed. I don't want to leave you any more than you want me to go, so your hesitation had to be for a reason.'

He followed her inside.

'Sorry. I'll move that pile of magazines so that you can sit down,' she apologised. 'Not quite as grand as your place, but it's the best I could manage on my salary and I'm just glad to be on the property ladder.'

'Do you believe in love at first sight?' he asked suddenly.

She felt a shudder run through her.

'I . . . well, I . . . '

'Because, ridiculous as it sounds, I think I'm in love with you, Megan.'

'Love? Me? You?' she burbled. 'Don't be silly. We hardly know each other. I mean . . . '

'What do you mean?' he asked.

'I don't know. Why me? You could choose from any woman anywhere. And yes, I certainly find you very attractive. But love?'

'I'm sorry. In my usual clumsy way, I'm rushing things. Jane's always telling me I'm too impulsive. I'd better go.'

'Cameron, we've only just met. How about we take some time to get to know each other?'

'Of course. You're absolutely right. But I'm scared of losing you just when I know for sure I've found the one person I want to spend my life with.'

'I think perhaps you *should* go,' she whispered, scarcely able to speak.

What was this gorgeous man saying? Was she dreaming or was it merely that too much wine was causing her to hallucinate?

He leaned over and kissed her. She felt as if she were flying high among the clouds.

'I'll call you tomorrow,' he promised. 'Sleep well.'

'I doubt I shall sleep a wink,' she said hoarsely. 'But thank you for a totally wonderful day.'

She watched as he drove away, then she slumped down on to her battered sofa, heart and mind racing. What to do? When it came to dreaming about finding the ideal man, Cameron Marshall ticked every box on her wish list.

★ ★ ★

When Megan arrived at work the next day, Lisa pounced on her. Don had clearly spread the word.

'Right,' said Lisa, grinning broadly, 'time to confess all! Don't move. Coffee is on its way.' She bounced over to the machine and came back with two cups.

'Clear off, Don. This is girl talk,' she commanded.

'I always know when I'm not wanted,' said Don, holding up his hands in mock surrender.

Megan poured out her story.

The look on Lisa's face was a picture of incredulity.

'He is truly gorgeous,' Megan said. 'And that house. Honestly, Lisa, I've never seen anywhere like it. It's simply heavenly. Perfect. Colour supplement material, all the way. Why on earth didn't I just fall into his arms before he changed his mind?'

'Because you are basically a sensible person who doesn't want to make a huge mistake, despite your scatty reputation,' Lisa replied. 'Mind you, you need to make your mind up fairly quickly or you might find I've grabbed him myself. If this chap is everything you say he is, I might just abandon Phil and go for it!'

Megan laughed, secure in the knowledge that she was being teased.

'But really, is there such a thing as love at first sight? Or is he feeding me a line because he thinks I'm a gullible idiot who'll fall for it? Actually, if I'm honest, I think I *am* more than a little in love with him already,' she said softly. It was a good feeling.

It was a long day and by the time she got back to her flat, she felt exhausted. What had she said just a few days ago? She wanted to liven up her personal life? Now her personal life was becoming so lively, it was almost running away from her and leaving her behind.

She took the last of her frozen ready-meals from the freezer and plonked it in the microwave.

There was a bang and a splutter, and all the lights went out leaving her staring in bewilderment at the machine. Then she realised what she'd done. She'd put the meal in the microwave in its foil dish. However much was this little lapse going to cost her?

The phone rang.

Crossing the room in the dark, she

crashed into the coffee table and only just managed to grab the phone before it hit the floor.

'Hello.'

'Megan. I didn't want to interrupt you at work, but I can't wait any longer to see you,' said Cameron's voice.

'OK,' she said.

'Actually, I refuse to take 'no' for an answer.'

His voice caressed her ear. The broken microwave, the fused lights, the fallen table didn't matter any more.

'OK,' she told him again.

'If you turn me down, I shall camp on your doorstep until you say 'yes'.'

'Aren't you listening? I said, OK.' She was beginning to giggle.

'And your doorstep is not the most comfortable place I have ever sat on. I'm not used to sharing a seat with two empty milk bottles and a pile of dead leaves.'

'The dead leaves, I can believe, but what makes you think there are two milk bottles on my doorstep?'

'An accurate guess? Or could I possibly be sitting there right at this moment?' he asked.

She went to the door of her flat and pulled it open. But, just as she'd thought, there were no milk bottles on the step.

She looked across the road.

In the light of the street lamps, she could see Cameron sitting on the step of one of the flats opposite.

He leapt to his feet at the sight of her and quickly crossed the road.

'I thought you lived at number six?'

'I do. But the number has fallen off the door. You were sitting outside number nine. That number only fell off at one end.'

He turned to look. The top screw had fallen out of the nine and the number had swung down to look like a six.

'But you were here last night! Didn't you realise you were at the wrong door?'

'I wasn't capable of taking in my surroundings last night. I only had eyes for you. Besides, I drove into the street from the other end.'

He looked slightly uncomfortable.

'Who lives there?' he asked anxiously, nodding towards number nine.

She grinned. 'A big beefy six-foot-four bloke. A nightclub bouncer by trade, I do believe.'

Cameron gulped.

'Let me in, quickly. Is he at home do you know?'

'I expect he's at work. Why, is something wrong?'

'I was shouting endearments through the letterbox. When I got no reply, I used my mobile. I might have had a narrow escape.'

He pushed past her into the flat and hid behind the door.

She burst out laughing.

'Why is it so dark in here?' he asked.

'I fused the lights. I was just about to find the trip switch when the phone rang.'

'You're priceless. You really do need someone to look after you. How did you fuse the lights?'

'Just used my own inimitable talents. What are you doing here anyhow?'

'I needed to see you. To talk something through with you.'

She was groping her way into the kitchen, hoping to find the torch she always kept handy. Except it wasn't in its usual place.

'Megan? Where have you gone?'

'I'm in the cupboard that passes for a kitchen in this shoe box. Not quite up to your standards. Drat,' she exclaimed. 'Now I've lost the matches as well as the torch.'

'You definitely need someone to look after you,' Cameron said, shaking his head in the darkness. 'You're not fit to be left alone. Keep talking and I'll find my way to you.'

'Stay there. You'll cause an accident.' She laughed. 'I'm a self-sufficient, capable woman. I'll prove it by . . . ' She paused, reaching into the meter cupboard. ' . . . switching the power back on, all by myself. There,' she said cheerfully. 'The lights are fixed.'

'Well done. Now, I'm starving,' Cameron said suddenly. 'Any chance you could feed me?'

She thought about the contents of her fridge and freezer and she knew there was nothing she could seriously offer him.

'Unless you like cheese on toast, we'd better go out.'

'Cheese on toast does have the advantage that we don't need to go out. Cheese on toast it is,' he agreed.

'In that case, I'll have to go out to buy some cheese. There's a little shop nearby. Won't be long.'

'Will you need bread as well?' he asked, a tinge of sarcasm in his voice.

'That's a point.' She grinned. 'And if you want coffee, I'd better buy some milk. In fact, I'd better check on the coffee as well.'

'Oh, my dear Megan. You're not housewife material, are you? Thank heavens we shall have dear old Mrs Baines, my housekeeper, to look after us after we're married.'

'Excuse me? Did I miss something? I don't remember ever agreeing to marry you. Or you asking me.'

Her comments were light-hearted, as indeed had been his own. But despite herself, she thrilled at the very notion of being married to this man. The whole idea was more than a little tempting.

'Actually, I think we will go out for dinner,' he said firmly. 'I don't think I want to risk your cooking if you're as hopeless as you make out! And promise me you'll get that microwave checked before you try to plug it in again.'

Megan felt another blush rising. She had hoped he wouldn't notice the strange effects produced on the foil dish that she had so stupidly put into the microwave.

'I didn't think you'd notice,' she said pulling a face.

★ ★ ★

They went to a small bistro near her flat and ate huge bowls of steaming pasta smothered in a delicious sauce.

'For someone so skinny, you have a pretty good appetite,' Cameron remarked as she wiped her plate clean with a piece of bread.

'It's all in the metabolism. I never put on weight.'

'Lucky old you. I suppose you don't need to work out, either.'

'Don't have time. I suppose you belong to some exclusive, upmarket gym just for young executives, and have a personal fitness trainer.'

'As a matter of fact, I don't need to. I have a small gym at home, down in the basement. It isn't finished yet but it soon will be.'

Megan stared. His own gym? Cameron Marshall lived on a different planet to her entirely.

'I need to keep myself in trim,' he told her. 'I entertain so much in the course of my business. I'd be in really bad shape if I didn't make some effort. But, enough about me. I want to ask you something.'

Megan looked troubled. After his comments about marriage, she wondered what was coming next.

'Go on then,' she whispered.

'Would you come on a little trip to France with me? I have to visit one or two small vineyards and I thought it would be the perfect opportunity for us to get to know each other better. It would give us plenty of time to talk. And I'd like you to meet some friends of mine who have a lovely old château in Burgundy.'

'It sounds heavenly,' Megan replied honestly. A few days in France with this man would be heaven.

'Great. That's all fixed then. We'll go on Monday. Or Sunday might be better.'

'You are joking, of course? I can't drop work just like that. Besides, I don't have any time off booked until August.'

'Well, if your boss won't give you the time off, then you'll just have to hand in your notice, then, won't you?' he suggested flippantly.

Megan felt angry. Although he was only joking, he was clearly used to getting what he wanted. She realised that, to be such a successful business man so young, he must have a ruthless streak. Warning bells began ringing in her head. So what was it about him that made her ignore every one of those bells?

'I might be able to get a couple of days off early next week,' she suggested. 'In which case, I could manage to get away for a long weekend.'

'We might as well go on Friday then, rather than wait until Saturday. I suggest we take a flight to Dijon late Friday afternoon. I'll arrange a hire car from the airport and we'll have a leisurely weekend. I can concentrate on work, Monday and Tuesday, then we can fly back Wednesday, if that suits you?'

It would suit her very well — so long as her boss would co-operate.

'I'll see James in the morning. He should be OK about me taking just a couple of days off. I'll call you.'

'I'll book everything, anyway. I can always cancel the arrangements if you can't get the time off. It's a pity you couldn't get longer, though. France is glorious at this time of year. I'll book us a couple of rooms in a hotel in Dijon for Friday night, and we'll go on to the Château early Saturday. Simone and Bertrand are looking forward to meeting you.'

'Are they?'

'I phoned them this afternoon to say you'd be coming with me. They're old friends. Small wine producers in the heart of the Burgundy region. You'll love it there.' His voice was full of enthusiasm.

'But you didn't even know that I'd go with you,' she protested.

'Oh, but I did. I knew you'd come, even if it took me all evening to persuade you. But they think we're staying with them for at least a week. Can't I persuade you to change your mind and come away for longer?'

Megan shook her head, a little troubled. She was such an independent person, and he seemed to be trying to take charge of her life.

A Proposal

They dawdled on the way back to her flat, hand in hand. At the door, he stopped, pulled her into his arms and kissed her. After a few minutes, he pushed her away very gently. 'You'd better go inside now. If I stay for a moment longer, I might never be able to leave. Don't forget to call me in the morning.'

He got back into his sleek silver car and drove away into the night.

Megan hugged her arms around herself, grinning with pure joy. She did not even consider that James, her boss, might refuse to give her time off. She was already planning what clothes she might take to France, and wondering if she had time to shop at lunch time the next day. There were sure to be extra things she needed.

Suddenly, she felt sure that her life

was about to change beyond all recognition. Then tiny fragments of common sense fought their way into her consciousness, making her calm down a little.

She knew she had been ready to be swept off her feet, but it was frightening how, in one short week, Cameron had come to dominate her life.

* * *

'You want some time off? You haven't given me much notice, have you?' grumbled James the next morning. 'What work have you got on?'

'Nothing very special. And I've been working late quite a lot recently.'

'Well, don't let these last-minute requests become a habit. I can't have everyone thinking they can just go off whenever they feel like a few days' break.'

'Thanks, James. You're a darling,' Megan said, whirling round to leave his office.

She called Cameron as soon as she got back to her desk. 'I've got some time off,' she said excitedly into the phone. 'Monday and Tuesday, but I have to be back Wednesday afternoon.'

'That's great,' Cameron replied, sounding rather cool, she thought. 'I'll speak to you later. Bye for now,' he said, hanging up.

The trouble with mobiles, Megan told herself, is that you never know where the person is when you call. He must have been in a meeting to be so unusually brusque.

But nothing was going to dampen her spirits. She worked fiendishly hard, clearing up all the work she had on hand so that James couldn't accuse her of leaving anything unfinished, even for two days.

At lunch time, she went shopping and bought various necessities. Staying in a château sounded very grand and she didn't want to let down either herself or Cameron. On her way back into the office she met Lisa, who was on her way out.

'You might have waited for me,' her

friend grumbled.

'Sorry! I had to do some emergency shopping. I'm off to France for a long weekend.'

'What?' squeaked Lisa. 'Not with The Handsome Hunk, surely?'

Megan nodded.

'Wow. You're a fast worker, once you make your mind up. I take it the wedding will be announced in all the best papers?'

'Don't count your chickens. This is only phase two — getting to know him better.' Megan's grin belied the note of caution in her words.

'Have a wonderful time. Just be careful. I've heard of love at first sight but never quite believed it. There can be skeletons in anyone's cupboard.'

'Don't be boring, Lisa. You may have found the love of your life, but I'm still looking.'

It was almost midnight by the time Megan got to bed that night, hoping she'd packed the right clothes for a weekend in a French château. It was an experience she was looking forward to with excitement, and more than a little trepidation.

★ ★ ★

She arrived at work early the next morning, but found it difficult to concentrate, and could hardly wait for the end of the day. Cameron phoned her during the morning to confirm the final arrangements, and told her that a car would collect her from the office at five o'clock to take her to the airport, where he would meet her before they caught their flight.

Four thirty. Four forty-five. Her heart beat faster each time she looked at her watch.

She went to the cloakroom to freshen up, watched by amused colleagues unused to seeing her behave this way.

At last, it was five o'clock, and she rushed down to reception and straight out of the front door to see if the car was waiting.

It was. With Cameron himself leaning against it.

Her heart turned over at the sight of him. He was wearing a lightweight linen suit in a subtle grey-blue colour. His dark hair was gleaming in the sun and he looked a picture of cool elegance.

Without a word, he opened the door for her, and helped her into the car while the driver took her bag and stowed it in the boot.

Then he leaned over and kissed her gently.

'You look lovely,' he murmured.

'Thanks. But I wasn't expecting to see you here,' she said.

'My meeting ended early, so I thought we might as well travel together. How about some champagne?'

He pulled open what looked like a cupboard, to reveal a small fridge. Inside the fridge, a bottle of Moët was chilled to perfection and he uncorked it expertly, spilling not the slightest drop.

He poured out a glass and handed it to her.

Then he took a small foil-wrapped package and opened it. 'Smoked salmon and asparagus rolls. Can't have you drinking on an empty stomach.'

She looked out of the window, scarcely noticing the lovely evening as they swept along towards the M4. The heavy traffic seemed to be in another dimension, quite separate from the back of the limousine.

She smiled at him, and he gazed back at her with a look of what could only be described as pure happiness. Then he took her fingers and gave them a gentle squeeze. It was enough to make her heart beat wildly.

They arrived at Heathrow with barely half an hour to spare before their flight, and were ushered into the First Class Lounge and offered more drinks.

Megan had only ever flown economy class, usually on family holidays, but she should have expected nothing less than the best with Cameron. She could enjoy getting used to this way of life, she thought to herself.

'I'll just have coffee, thanks,' she said to the steward.

It seemed no time at all before they had boarded the flight and Megan sank back into the deep seat. She was loving every minute of her VIP treatment. Cameron brushed past her as he sat in his own seat, and she caught a whiff of his aftershave, subtle and fresh.

★ ★ ★

Cameron had driven them to the hotel in Dijon in a hire car and, from her room, Megan could see the creamy yellow buildings that were deepening in colour in the lowering sun.

She showered and changed into a simple linen dress, picking up a silky shawl as she left her room in case it was cool later. She knocked on Cameron's door to let him know that she was ready.

'I hope you haven't planned anything too grand. My wardrobe is rather limited,' she said, feeling almost shy.

'You look perfect,' he reassured her. 'I thought we'd take a short walk and have dinner in one of my very favourite restaurants. Have you been here before?'

'No. I've been to France, but not to this region.'

He smiled, took her hand and led her out into the busy town.

They spent an hour wandering round small streets and broad boulevards and it seemed as if every resident of the city was doing the same thing.

'I'm starving,' she said eventually. 'Where's this special restaurant of yours?'

'Right here. We have a table reserved and I have ordered the regional specialities.'

'I could eat a banquet and still have room,' she said happily.

Then began a routine which set the pattern for the weekend.

When they walked into the restaurant there was a great cry from Monsieur le Patron, followed by a great deal of embracing and a torrent of French that meant nothing to her and left her gaping in bewilderment.

Then a large woman in an apron appeared and the whole business was repeated. Somewhere in the middle of these proceedings, Megan was introduced and given her own rapturous welcome. At last, they were ushered to a table to one side of the busy room. Kir Royales were brought to them and she sipped the luscious champagne and blackcurrant.

Various acquaintances of Cameron's, including staff from the kitchen, came over to say hello during the meal and, encouraged by the enormously friendly welcome, Megan gave her schoolgirl French an airing.

Cameron smiled his approval as she made the effort to communicate.

It was after one o'clock in the morning when they returned to the hotel.

'You made quite a hit,' Cameron said with obvious pleasure. 'I suppose you gathered they were all wishing us a happy married life.'

'What?' Megan gasped. 'They think we're getting married? Whatever gave them that idea?'

'It must have been the adoring glances you were giving me all evening. Although I did mentioned in passing that we were thinking about it. But you know what the French are like where romance is concerned. Now, I promise. I won't mention it again.'

'OK,' Megan said. 'But I wondered what you've told your friends? Simone and Bertrand? I hope they won't be expecting us to name dates?'

'Don't worry about it. They are very polite and wouldn't dream of making you feel in the least embarrassed. Well, here we are,' he said as they reached the corridor outside their rooms. 'I'll call you in the morning so we can have breakfast together. We don't need to be up at the crack of dawn but we don't want to waste the day. Goodnight.'

He leaned over and, putting a finger

under her chin, kissed her gently on the lips.

★ ★ ★

She awoke to the sound of the telephone shrilling and sat up, rubbing her eyes and wondering where on earth she was. Her head felt muzzy with the wine and the late night. She glanced at the clock and was amazed to see that it was already ten o'clock. She reached out and picked up the phone.

'Come on, lazybones. You're wasting a perfect day. Breakfast is waiting for you in my room. You have five minutes before I call the manager to break down your door.'

Without even waiting for her to reply, Cameron put down the phone.

Five minutes? No problem. She rarely had much more time than that to get ready on any weekday morning.

A quick shower and then she dressed, all well within her allotted time. There were no lengthy debates with herself about what to wear as she had brought so little with her. Cream linen slacks and a chocolate shirt were pulled on, and a brush pulled through her tangled curls.

She knocked at Cameron's door and he let her in.

'A woman who really can get ready quickly. Come and eat.'

He gestured towards a trolley set out with a typical continental breakfast and a vacuum jug of coffee.

'I couldn't eat a thing,' she moaned, looking longingly at the fresh croissants. 'I ate so much yesterday, I shall take days to get over it.'

'Come now. You're too skinny by half.' He poured her some coffee and placed a croissant on her plate. 'Go on. Just one.'

'I don't usually eat breakfast,' she admitted.

'Don't have time, I expect. You really do need looking after.'

He gazed at her, willing her to eat. After the first tentative nibble, she quickly finished the rest of the delicious pastry.

Cameron grinned. 'I knew you wouldn't be able to resist.'

* * *

It was almost lunchtime when they arrived at Château Duras. It was a grey, stone-built house, topped with shiny, almost black tiles. There were two round towers, one at each end, making it look like a child's picture book version of a French château but it was, despite the rather grand frontage, a very comfortable family home. The once elegant furnishings were rather faded, and many of the carpets almost threadbare in places, but it all added to the lived-in quality that gave the place such charm.

'We were thrilled when Cameron told us you would accompany him on this trip,' Simone Duras said softly, her English impeccable, as she showed Megan to her room. 'I'll leave you to settle in,' she said with a smile. 'Lunch is ready whenever you are. Just a simple meal and it's cold, so nothing will spoil.'

Megan felt instantly at home and sensed that she and Simone could become friends.

She unpacked her few belongings and hung her two dresses in the huge wardrobe, wondering if she'd brought enough clothes with her.

After freshening up in the en-suite bathroom that had been cunningly constructed to one side of the room, she went along the landing to knock at Cameron's door.

He smiled as he opened it. 'Are you ready for lunch?'

She nodded and they went down the enormous oak staircase together.

'We'll take you on a tour of the estate this afternoon,' suggested Bertrand as they ate. 'If you'd like that, of course. I know Cameron is anxious to see how the vines are doing. He likes to take a look before he orders our entire output.

Now, let me fill your glass, Megan. I think you are going to like this. One of our lighter wines suitable for lunch.'

Megan began to see just how little she knew about wine. She could recognise the names of those her father liked and bought regularly, but apart from that she was a complete novice.

* * *

Throughout the day, Cameron was attentive. On one occasion, when she had wandered a little way from the others during the tour, she realised they were all speaking French together. Cameron was fluent but whenever she was with them, they spoke only English.

She warmed even more to the French couple and their beautiful manners. The scent of the grape flowers filled her senses. It seemed impossible to think of these actual vines producing wine that would be sent all over the world. Mile upon mile of carefully cultivated plants were stretched across their wire supports. The amount of work to tie them and prune them must have been tremendous.

She could hardly imagine this elegant couple spending so many hours toiling in the fields, but they told her that they worked together to produce their crop with only the minimum of help.

★   ★   ★

Megan's precious few days in France whirled by. She and Cameron visited vineyards and small châteaux, and went on a trip into the beautiful historic town of Beaune. They did all the touristy things, even though she was certain it must have been the umpteenth time for him. He knew all the right places to go and things to see. He knew the history of everything, from the old Hospice, to the miles of wine caves under the town. He assured her that seeing them with her was as good as seeing them for the first time himself.

They sampled the wines . . . Gevrey Chambertin . . . Nuits-St Georges and dozens of others. Hesitating at times in case he was boring her, Cameron gave her small pointers to the flavour, the texture and the nuances that made each of them unique.

As they drove through the villages that gave their names to these famous wines, Megan's mind whirled.

'I didn't realise that all these places were anything more than names on wine labels,' she murmured. 'It makes such a difference, seeing the grapes actually growing. If ever Dad buys any of these wines I shall be able to tell him that I actually saw the grapes growing.'

'We'll make a connoisseur of you yet.' Cameron laughed. 'Now, the grapes they use in this region are mostly Pinot Noir,' he continued and set about telling her all about them.

She wondered whether to ask him to help her write an article on wine production, maybe even a series of articles.

'And are you familiar with all the regions of France?' she asked.

'Only a few of them. There are some nice little areas north of the Rhone Valley. If only we had more time, we could drive down there and I could show you some of them.' His enthusiasm for his subject was most appealing and Megan felt she could sit beside him, listening to him talk, forever.

'Next time, perhaps.'

'Now that does sound encouraging,' he said, smiling at her. 'Jane tells me I go on a bit but, if you are suggesting another trip, it can't have been all bad.'

* * *

All too soon, it was their last night in France. Bertrand had organised a celebration meal at a small restaurant situated in the village closest to the château. It was within walking distance and Megan, Cameron and their host and hostess all strolled down companionably in the clear evening air.

'This is such a lovely place,' Megan said to Simone. 'I shall always remember these few days. It's been perfect. Thank you.'

The older woman gave her hand a squeeze.

'Please, come and see us again. Your parents would be most welcome, too. Cameron has told us that your father is one of his good customers. You have shops I understand?'

'Just a few small grocery stores with off-licences. The old-fashioned sort, where personal service and quality still count.'

'And you are not tempted to be a part of the family business?'

'Heavens, no. I'm a journalist. But my brother works with my father.'

It was a happy evening with superb food, wine and excellent company.

'I can't believe that, this time tomorrow, I shall be back with microwave meals for one,' Megan said with a wry grin.

'Always providing that you get the

microwave fixed,' Cameron reminded her.

She pulled a face. Her flat seemed to belong to another life entirely.

They walked back to the château through the balmy night air. It was a perfect evening with bright stars shining from a clear sky. The outline of the lovely old buildings gave a sense of fairy tale to the whole setting. Cameron held Megan's fingers loosely as they walked.

'This is such a beautiful place,' she whispered softly.

'It is quite magical. I trust this weekend has been everything you hoped for?'

'And more,' she whispered.

'Does that mean that, like me, you've begun to believe in love at first sight?'

'Perhaps. But it's all a bit unreal. Like a story that might end on the next page before it really gets going in the first place.'

'I assure you, my dearest Megan, that there is no way I will let our story end before it has scarcely begun. These few days have convinced me. You are the woman I've been waiting for and I hope that you will soon realise that marrying me is the right thing to do. I love you.'

Megan laughed nervously. He was becoming far too serious, far too fast.

'We've only known each other for a few days and you're suggesting you know me well enough to want to get married? I think I want to enjoy getting to know you properly first.'

'Fair enough. But don't make me wait too long. I couldn't bear it. I'm not indecisive like you.'

'Indecisive?' she squeaked, laughing as they all went inside.

★ ★ ★

At breakfast the next day, Megan gave a deep sigh. 'It's been fantastic staying here. Thank you so much, Simone.'

'We've enjoyed having you here. We always enjoy seeing Cameron and, now you are with him, it's even better. Give our love to Jane, will you?' Simone told them both.

'You could always change your mind and stay on, Megan,' Cameron suggested. 'If anyone grumbles, hand in your notice.' His voice was quietly confident.

She sat up straight, slightly angry that he didn't seem to take her commitment to her career seriously.

'I love my work. There's no way I'd leave on a whim.'

'OK. Don't let's spoil our break with a petty argument. If you insist, then I'll make sure that you're back in your office by this afternoon. But it's a pity. We could have had a celebration lunch with Simone and Bertrand.'

'Celebrating what?' Bertrand asked.

'I think we may be announcing our engagement very soon.'

'Now hang on a minute,' Megan protested.

'You can have as many minutes as

you wish,' said Cameron softly, 'but there's no point in holding out against the inevitable, Megan, my darling.'

She didn't know whether or not he was joking.

Naming The Day

'There's nothing wrong, is there?' Simone asked Megan after Cameron and Bertrand had left the room to collect the luggage. 'You look worried.'

'I *am* worried. Quite apart from the way that Cameron is determined to sweep me off my feet, I don't think he realises how important my work is to me. I had to fight to get where I am and I can't just give it all up.'

'He'll come round, I'm sure. He is a very masculine man. He wants to do the whole hunter-gatherer thing. He needs to provide for you so that you want for nothing.' She smiled knowingly. 'The trick is to let husbands think they are in control, but all the time you organise things the way *you* want. Believe me, when you know him better you will soon discover how to wrap him around your finger and to achieve what you want. It's what all we women have to learn when we marry.'

'But you and Bertrand are equal partners in everything you do, surely?' Megan asked in surprise.

'Yes, but we have been married for many years. I have taken a long time to achieve exactly what I want. We're both happy with it.'

Then Cameron came down with the suitcases and the farewells began.

At last they were driving away from the delightful château.

'This past few days have been like a fairy tale,' she said happily.

'The first of many such occasions. I think we should look around the shops at the airport, and I'll buy you something wonderful, to mark the occasion.'

A ring? wondered Megan. Her heart raced. If he was going to buy her a ring, that would make the decision for her. In spite of all her misgivings at the way Cameron was rushing her into this relationship, she thrilled at the idea of flashing an extravagant engagement ring around the office.

But it wasn't to a jewellers' but to a clothes shop that Cameron guided her.

'I thought you might like something special to wear at our engagement party,' he said happily. 'It'll be taking place at my house on Saturday — if you're not doing anything else? Why the surprised face? We are getting engaged, aren't we?'

'Well, I suppose we could!' she said, laughing. 'Just engaged, though. I need some time to get used to the idea of being engaged before I agree to set the date for a wedding. And when did you decide all this about a party?'

'Two minutes ago. Leave it all to me. If you did the food we'd be stuck with microwave dinners for each guest. I'll organise caterers, and wine's hardly a problem, is it?'

Megan laughed but had to suppress a little shiver. What she had thought to be light-hearted banter was snowballing out of control.

'Come on. Which of these gorgeous outfits would the future Mrs Marshall like to choose?'

She looked at the array of designer labels in front of her and felt totally overwhelmed. Normally, she loved buying clothes but, at this moment, too much was happening too quickly.

'Cameron,' she said suddenly. 'Cameron, I can't do this now. My mind is buzzing and I can't make rational decisions, and these clothes are lovely, but too expensive to choose from in a hurry.'

'What an extraordinary woman you are. Most women I know would give their eye teeth for a designer dress.'

'I'm not most women,' she said fiercely.

'Which is precisely why I love you and want to marry you. Come on, then. Let's go and find somewhere to eat.'

Megan groaned. 'Not more food,' she said. 'Let's just walk a little,' she suggested. 'I never want to eat again for at least a month.'

'Just think. We could be married by then,' he said cheerfully.

She shook her head. 'I have to talk to my parents. They don't even know we've been seeing each other, let alone this latest piece of news.'

He suddenly stood stock-still and stared at her for several seconds.

'You sound so boringly practical, I could almost believe I've misjudged you. And there I was, thinking you specialised in organising muddles.'

Her face remained serious, despite his attempt to joke.

'It's quite likely that you *have* misjudged me. Let's face it, Cameron, we hardly know anything about each other. Perhaps we are making a mistake.'

She looked away, feeling suddenly emotional.

'You're over-tired,' he told her, taking her arm and walking on. 'Expect to find me waiting for you at my home on Friday, after work. I doubt I'll survive two whole days without you as it is.

And don't forget to buy something special to wear on Saturday. But you must give me the bill, I insist.'

'You can insist all you like, but I can just about afford my own dress for my own party.'

'Must you always be so independent? Please, let me spoil you a bit. It's my right as a doting fiancé. Buy something sensational.' He took her hand and squeezed it. 'Everything is going to work out. Don't worry, my darling. In fact, you never need worry again, about anything.'

When she arrived back in London, Megan found it quite surreal to walk into the familiar buzz of office noise after waking that morning in France.

She sat at her desk, leafing through a pile of messages. If she could find a moment during that afternoon, she really must phone her parents. But all too soon, it was six o'clock and she was nearly collapsing with weariness.

She hadn't even caught up with the gossip with Lisa, but it was always like that on the day before press day.

When she finally got home, she fell asleep on her sofa as soon as she sat down. So she crawled into bed and slept soundly until morning.

* * *

'Have you got time for a chat? I still haven't heard about your trip to France. How did it go?' called Lisa as she walked into the office the next day.

She made her way over to Megan's desk and peered into her face. 'Gosh! You look awful.'

'Thanks,' retorted Megan. 'Just what I wanted to hear. Actually, I feel utterly exhausted after too many late nights and too much rich food and wine. And I practically slept the clock round last night.'

'So?' her friend demanded. 'How was the trip?'

'Fabulous. The château was in the most heavenly part of France, and Simone and Bertrand were lovely.'

'Don't be so evasive. You know what I want to hear. How was The Handsome Hunk.'

'You'll have to stop referring to my fiancé by that stupid name.'

Lisa gave a squeal.

'Oh, Megan, that's so exciting! A bit sudden, though! We must go out to celebrate tonight, after work. I'll get everyone organised.'

'No, Lisa, please. I must get an early night, tonight. But we're having a proper engagement party on Saturday evening and everyone's invited.'

Lisa snatched at her left hand and stared.

'So, where's the expensive engagement ring? I'd have expected a massive solitaire at the very least.'

'Haven't had time to look for a ring, yet. I expect we'll buy it on Saturday, before the party. You'll see it then. Now, I must get on with some work.'

Later that morning, Megan plucked up the courage to phone her parents.

She knew exactly what her mother

would say — that it was all too hasty — and that was exactly the reaction that she got.

'But I love him, Mum. I do truly love him. He's everything I've ever wanted in a man. I'm not a kid any more. I'm twenty-five, for goodness' sakes, and I've lived in London for three years. No. Marrying Cameron is not a mistake. I am absolutely certain.'

'Now, who is trying to convince who, I wonder?' Mona said softly. 'When are you coming home so that we can sit and talk about this properly?'

'Well, that's the next thing I was about to tell you. We're having a party on Saturday night at Cameron's house. You'll love his home, Mum. It's the most beautiful house I've ever seen — everything has been restored with such care and good taste.'

'And who was responsible for that? Cameron's sister, I guess. And she will be living with you, I take it? Assuming you're going to live there after you're married? And it will be a long journey from there to your work in London, or are you intending to giving up your job?'

'Don't spoil it, Mum. I'm so happy. Let me be happy for a while and save the questions until later.'

By the end of the call, Megan felt totally drained of the little energy she had left. Her mother had given voice to all the concerns and doubts that she was trying to push from her own mind.

There was Jane for a start. How would it be to share a house with someone else, especially when newly married? She thought of the difficulties — having time to themselves, and who would actually run the place?

★ ★ ★

At lunch time she went for a sandwich with Lisa and they talked about her worries. But Lisa was ever the optimist.

'I think it's all just brilliant. So romantic. I wish a rich, handsome young man would become besotted

82

with me and whisk me away to his mansion.'

When they arrived back in the office, Megan's desk had disappeared beneath a huge bouquet.

'Wow! Get a look at those,' Lisa exclaimed. 'What it is to get engaged to a wealthy man. Does he have a brother by any chance?'

'They're not from him. They're from his sister, or so the card says. Delighted to welcome you to the family. Love, Jane. That's nice, isn't it?'

Lisa nodded. She was thrilled for her friend, but just the tiniest bit jealous of her good fortune.

'So, what are you wearing on Saturday night?'

'Oh, crumbs. I forgot. I'm supposed to be wearing something sensational which I still have to go out and buy. When can I fit that in, I wonder?'

'Late night shopping? I'd come with you but I'm going out this evening.'

The rest of the staff had already congratulated Megan on her engagement and several of them had said they'd be coming to the party.

Fortunately, she was able to sneak away from the office a little early, and managed to find the perfect dress on her way home. In her favourite shade of sea-green, it showed off her figure to its best advantage, but she winced when she saw the price ticket. Perhaps she would allow Cameron to pay for it after all.

When she got home, there were four messages on her answerphone. One was from her mother sounding worried, asking her to ring back, and the other three messages were from Cameron. The first to say he loved her, the second asking her to call and tell him what she was doing on August first.

In the third message he asked if she'd had dinner yet. She smiled and dialled his number as her first priority.

'Where have you been until this time?' he demanded. 'I was about to send out a search party.'

'In reply to your first message, I love you, too. To your second message, I don't know what I'm doing on August the first. And to the third message, no, I haven't eaten yet.'

'Glad about the first. Second: you're getting married. Third: beans on toast will do. If you have any beans. Or bread.'

She laughed.

'This is getting silly. No way am I getting married on August the first. It's less than a month away. Don't be ridiculous.'

'We'll discuss it tomorrow evening. What time will you be here? I'll meet you at the station.'

They chatted for some time about arrangements for the party, until she suddenly remembered all the things she was supposed to do before she left for the office the next morning.

'I must go now or I shall have to come back here after work tomorrow.'

As soon as she had hung up, she picked up the phone again to call her mother. Doubtless Mona wanted to talk some more about her daughter's startling news. She might also be hoping to persuade Megan to postpone the engagement party. But after talking to Cameron again, Megan felt much more certain and secure about the way her relationship with him was going.

'Megan, thank heavens you called back. Your father and I are both worried sick. We've been discussing everything. We really do need to talk to you, darling. We must see you as soon as possible. Please come home tomorrow and let's talk it through.'

'I'm going to be at work all day tomorrow, and then I'm going to Cameron's in the evening. I'll see you on Saturday at the party. You will come, won't you? Why not come early, in the afternoon, and then we can talk? And you can see Cameron's fabulous house before everyone else arrives.'

Mona listened to her daughter's chatter. Much as she had liked Cameron on the one and only occasion she'd met him, and much as she wanted to see Megan settled, she sensed this was wrong. It was all too hasty. But she knew better than to challenge her head-strong daughter. If she put obstacles in the way, it was more likely to drive Megan into Cameron's arms.

Mona drew a deep breath and, much against her better judgment, she said, 'All right, darling. We'll be there early afternoon, providing Dad can get away, of course.'

'I'm so happy, Mum. I never believed something like this could ever happen to me. I never believed in love at first sight but I'm totally converted.'

Mona listened to her daughter's excited chatter. Long may it last, she hoped, but she was deeply concerned. Megan had always been impulsive but this was something quite different. This was too important to joke about. She must talk it through with her husband. He'd be able to find out more about Cameron from his business acquaintances.

Cameron Marshall was altogether too perfect, too rich and much too good-looking.

★ ★ ★

What was left of that evening, Megan spent packing essentials for the weekend.

As she worked, she was struck by several exciting little thoughts; the first of which was the realisation that, if she would be regularly spending time at Cameron's, she would need to leave a set of basics at his house so that she needn't keep packing and unpacking. She must buy a few extras with that in mind.

Then, looking round at the tiny flat that had been her home for the past three years, she realised that once she was married, she would no longer need it.

And what of her job? Could she really continue to work in London and travel so far each day? If she had a normal nine to five job it would be easier, but she had to work late on so many evenings, and often had to work away.

But none of this mattered for the moment. She knew that what she wanted most in the world was to be with Cameron.

★ ★ ★

The first thing Megan saw when she arrived in the office the next morning was a note from James, commanding her to go to see him as soon as possible.

'I understand congratulations are in order,' he said, much to her surprise as she walked into his office.

'Yes. Thank you. We hope you will come to the engagement party tomorrow. I'm sorry it's rather short notice, but it's all happened so quickly.'

James nodded at her. He looked thoughtful.

'And do you propose to continue working here after you're married?'

'Well, yes. Of course I do. Why wouldn't I?'

'People change. Women especially. Babies and all that? Well, I hope you know what you're doing.'

He nodded to indicate the interview was at an end.

Megan returned to her desk, annoyed. James was being sexist. He was making assumptions about her. Babies and all that. How dare he? She stood still. Babies. She had no idea how Cameron felt about children.

She had always supposed she would have children one day. But she'd barely grasped the implications of getting married, let alone the whole family thing.

She was overwhelmed by a vast wave of panic. A wedding on August the first? It was quite out of the question. Cameron must be reasonable. Why he had to be in quite such a hurry was something of a mystery. Maybe she should be flattered that he was so in love with her.

*　　*　　*

Mona seemed unusually shy and quiet when she and Megan's father arrived at

Cameron's home on Saturday afternoon. Charles looked even more tired than he had on the last occasion Megan had seen him.

She was concerned about how pale he looked, and made a mental note to ask her mother if there really was something wrong.

The relationship between Cameron and her father had changed. Cameron called her father 'sir' a couple of times, which made Megan giggle. She teased him about it, suggesting the two men might need to go into a huddle to discuss 'honourable intentions' and 'prospects for the future'.

'So, are you going to show us round?' her father was asking. 'It's a fine place you have here. What's the history?'

Cameron and Charles went off together, talking about the house and what had been done to it. Mona was interested, naturally, but she was more concerned about her daughter.

'You are sure it's what you want?' she asked. 'Marriage to Cameron?'

Megan nodded.

'I must say, I can see why you were swept off your feet. You should have seen the flowers he and Jane sent to me after the dinner party. He's thoroughly charming and this house . . . well, what can one say? But remember, darling, however rich he is and however comfortable his home, marriage is a very serious commitment. No amount of money can compensate for unhappiness. Always is a long time, as I have so often said.'

'Mum, it isn't how you think. I haven't been dazzled by his wealth and by all the attention he's been showering on me. I love him, Mum. And, even although he's out of my league, I'm certain he loves me, though I can't think why.'

'Because you are a lovely girl and that's not just your proud mother talking. Well, if you're quite certain that this marriage is what you want, then we'll support you all the way. I'm concerned only for your happiness. Be funny if Ewan and Jane hit it off as well, wouldn't it? I haven't seen either of them since we arrived, have you?'

'No. But I gather little brother has had the odd date or two with my future sister-in-law.'

Megan still found it strange to think of herself as a married woman.

'What about an engagement ring? Are you going to bother, or are you just going to have a wedding ring? I should have thought you would have a ring if you're going to have a party to celebrate the occasion.'

Megan had been a little disappointed that Cameron hadn't mentioned a ring. She'd even asked, unsubtly, if they were going shopping that morning.

He'd asked if there was something special she needed and she'd said no.

Then Cameron and Charles came back into the room, looking relaxed.

Mona examined her husband's face, as if she was trying to read something from his expression.

'Is there anything I can do to help

with the party?' she asked. 'How many people are you expecting?'

Cameron gave a shrug.

'We're not really sure. It's been a case of an open-house invitation. I think Megan said there would be about twenty from her work and I've asked a number of friends and business people. It's a very special occasion. I suppose there will be around a hundred all told.'

Mona gasped. A hundred people, just to the engagement party? And at short notice! What on earth would the wedding be like?

'The caterers are arriving at six so there really is nothing to do. Perhaps you'd like a tour of the house?'

They left the room talking earnestly, leaving father and daughter alone.

'Is it your turn to ask me if I know what I'm doing?' Megan said to Charles. They both laughed before he pulled her into a hug and said how proud he was of her.

'Are you all right, Dad? You look a bit pale. I hope you haven't been overdoing it more than usual.'

He laughed again and said he needed to work hard if he was to keep up with all of this, waving his hand around him.

'You've certainly done very well for yourself, darling.'

'It's Cameron I love, not his home or possessions,' she said a little stiffly.

'I should hope so, too,' he replied, patting her gently on the shoulder. 'For such a young man he's achieved so much.'

* * *

The party seemed to go on for ever. Megan began to feel totally confused about all the new people she was meeting, and her arm ached from shaking hands. After the buffet supper, a toast was proposed to the newly engaged couple by a guest who'd been introduced to her as Gavin, Cameron's oldest friend.

When Cameron stood up to reply, he drew Megan close and handed her a small leather box that looked slightly battered. She stared at it and at him.

'Well, go on. Open it.'

With trembling fingers, she lifted the lid.

Inside, on a bed of white satin, was a ring — an enormous emerald in an antique gold setting. She gasped and stood speechless, staring at the exquisite jewel.

'I hope you like it, darling. It belonged to my grandmother and then to my mother. It seemed appropriate that you should inherit it.'

'Oh, Cameron, I love it. It's quite beautiful.'

She felt tears of joy burning behind her eyes. She could not have chosen a better ring if she had searched through every jeweller's in the country.

Cameron's speech was brief and to the point.

'Thank you all for coming, especially at such short notice, and we hope to see you all again at the wedding. Megan seems to think August the first is too soon, so I am prepared to wait until the seventh.'

Everyone clapped and cheered and their health was drunk yet again.

Mona stood quietly to one side, looking very worried. She had hoped they would at least take time to get to know each other with a long engagement. August the seventh. Only a month away. Apart from her fear that her daughter was marrying in haste and would repent her mistake at leisure, as the bride's parents, the burden on the Belmores would be considerable.

It wasn't just the cost but the organisation of it all. If tonight was anything to go by, lavish would be an understatement.

Mona felt positively weak at the knees at the thought of what lay ahead. She would have to enlist Jane's help. Megan would be of little practical use. She would probably be so wound up with her own agenda that the next few weeks would bring quite enough problems of their own.

Then she gave a little smile. Looking at the newly engaged pair she could see only happiness shining from them. Perhaps it was going to be all right. Megan had certainly made the catch of the county.

'You really do like the ring, don't you darling?' Cameron asked, when all the guests had finally left. 'You have only to say if you don't and I'll get you something else. I wanted you to have this one but if you prefer something else, I wouldn't mind. Honestly.'

'I love it, Cameron, truly.'

'The emerald matches your eyes,' he said softly. 'It even takes up the colour of your dress, which I also love by the way.'

'You're sure Jane doesn't mind me having it? The ring I mean. Girls usually inherit their mother's jewellery, don't they?'

'She doesn't like emeralds much, so there's no problem. Now, I think we need to call it a day before we drop with exhaustion.'

He kissed her on her lips, a gentle kiss.

★ ★ ★

The following morning, Megan awoke early and lay thinking. It was only two weeks since she'd first met Cameron at her parents' dinner party. Last weekend they were in Burgundy and now, here she was, engaged, with the wedding day itself fixed.

One never knew what lay around any corner.

She spent a lazy Sunday with Cameron, reading papers, drinking coffee and walking in the extensive gardens. All too soon, it was time for her to return to London and her work.

'I'm in town on Tuesday and Thursday this week. We can meet if you like,' Cameron said. 'Or I could come to your flat. What would you want to do? Dinner? A film? Or we could go to a show?'

'Oh, Cameron, I'm working late on

Tuesday evening. I'm sorry. I've got to go to an editorial meeting.'

'You are engaged to *me*, for heavens' sake,' Cameron said, thunder in his voice.

Megan felt the colour draining from her face. She took a deep breath to control herself.

'This is my job. It's what I do. I'm sorry if you don't like it but you'll just have to get used to it.'

Cameron stared at her, his own anger rising.

To Megan's great relief, he forced a smile.

'Sorry. You're right, of course. Now, I'd better drive you to the station if you're absolutely determined to return to London tonight.'

He gritted his teeth together as his mind shrieked out to him: *No. Not again. It mustn't happen again.*

'We've had our first row,' Megan said unhappily. 'I hope we've made it up properly before I leave.'

'Of course. How could I be angry

with you for long? I love you far too much for that.'

'Don't let my work come between us,' she pleaded.

'I wouldn't dream of it,' Cameron replied, a smile on his handsome face. 'I have no intention of letting anything come between us, ever. Now, the station?'

Wedding Nerves

At work on Monday morning, Lisa was filled with praise for the party. 'You lucky thing,' she told Megan. 'Fancy having that gorgeous hunk of a man all to yourself. And that house. Did you ever in your wildest dreams think you'd end up living somewhere like that?'

'Come on, Lisa. I'm still me. And I shall expect you to be a bridesmaid at this wedding. I need someone to bring me down to earth.'

Lisa gave one of her squeals of delight.

'I'd be delighted. Me and who else?'

'Sorry?'

'Well, who else is destined to get togged up in fancy clothes and trail after you? I guess there'll be the full blown affair with a stream of little pageboys and bridesmaids.'

'Good lord, no. I mean, it will

probably be just you and Jane, if she agrees. I don't want anything ostentatious. In fact, if it was up to me, the guest list would be just you and Jane, Cameron and my parents and brother.'

'Get real, Megan. Someone with Cameron's money and background is going to want the wedding of the century. Thanks, love, anyway, for asking me to be a bridesmaid. I accept and would have lynched you if you hadn't asked. I must get on now or the big white chief will be after me.'

Megan chewed her pen thoughtfully. She hadn't had time to think very much about the wedding itself, but she didn't want some elaborate society do. It was the day she was to marry Cameron. That was the important thing. It was not an excuse to show off to hoards of people she didn't even know.

Obviously, they needed to sit down and thrash out the plans. What had he said? August the seventh? In that case, the simpler the wedding, the better.

* * *

It seemed that Megan would not get her wish. When she got home from work that evening, the answering machine had been working overtime. There were several calls from her mother and several more from Cameron. Each call seemed to contradict the previous until she was totally confused.

She spoke to Cameron first. He told her not to worry as he had several discussions about the wedding with her mother and everything was now sorted. They had agreed upon the date, the church and the venue, and all she had to do was to turn up on the day looking gorgeous.

She felt her stomach begin to twist into a tight knot of tension. Once again, everything was spinning out of control.

To avoid an argument, she said she had to go.

She took several deep breaths before she called her mother.

'Hello, darling,' Mona said happily. 'I've had such nice chats with Cameron today. He really is very charming. Your father and I so much enjoyed the party and we are very happy for you. I think Cameron and I covered most things on the phone this afternoon. You can ignore all the messages.'

'There *is* one thing you seem to have forgotten about. Me. Did either of you consider what I want? I am the bride. Without me, you don't even have a wedding to organise.'

'You don't mean you've changed your mind? Oh, surely not! Megan, you can't be having second thoughts already?'

'Oh, no. I want to marry Cameron. But it would have been nice to have been consulted about the wedding arrangements! What about the guest list?'

'Well, that's obvious, isn't it? Your father and Cameron are both business men. They'll need to invite clients, colleagues etc. Then there are friends and relations. It's going to be a pretty extensive list. I thought Madge's twins would make delightful pageboys and then . . . ' she continued to rattle on about long-lost cousins and second cousins, all of whom had the right to expect to be attendants, until Megan's head was whirling.

'I'm having Lisa from work as a bridesmaid and maybe Jane, if she's OK with that,' Megan interrupted. 'And that's all. I'm not having a string of hyperactive children behaving badly all day. I'd like a small, simple affair with as little fuss as possible.'

'But, Megan, you can't! We've already ordered the invitations. As it is, the printer is doing Dad a favour to get them done at such short notice. And Cameron's being marvellous. He's organising the caterers again — the same people you had for the party — and he's organising the drinks, of course. And he's insisting on paying for everything. Mind you, Dad and I shall expect to chip in quite substantially. Whatever else, we'll pay for your dress and the bridesmaids' and pageboys' outfits.'

Megan held the phone away from her ear. Her mother was in full flow and nothing was going to stop her. As soon as she paused for breath, Megan interrupted again.

'And where is this spectacle going to take place? Have you worked that out too?'

'At Cameron's house, of course. Ours is much too small. We shall hire a marquee. It's the perfect setting and Cameron thinks he can organise the village church so you have only a short drive. Oh, and he's organising the marquee hire. Someone he knows. They do gilt chairs and tables and a lining for the tent so it looks really special. I thought the pink sounded nicest. Yellow might make you look too sallow.'

'Will I be saying my own lines on the day? Or maybe you'll have organised someone to do that for me as well?'

'Megan, darling, I thought you'd be pleased to have all the bother taken off your hands. All you have to do is come home at the weekend and be fitted for your dress. I've had a word with Mrs Davies. She's agreed to make you something special. She's wonderful. Expensive, but she's worth it.'

'For heaven's sake, Mum! At least let me choose my own dress. And I want a say in what my two bridesmaids are wearing. Get on with your lists and whatever you like but leave me and the bridesmaids to do our own thing. And for heavens' sake, don't lumber me with a horde of little kids to traipse after me down the aisle.'

'But I've already phoned your Aunt Madge and I'm phoning the rest later. You can still have your friend from work, and Jane. But the photographs will look so much nicer if there's a group. And remember how much you enjoyed being a bridesmaid to Aunt Madge, when you were little? It seems a nice idea for us to reciprocate.'

Megan sighed. She did not doubt that this would be the first of many such conversations.

'Then you'd better phone and un-reciprocate, Mum. I mean it. I have to go now.'

She felt tears burning. She glowered at the ring on her left hand. Why did a wedding have to be so complicated? All she wanted was Cameron.

★ ★ ★

For the rest of her life, Megan would remember the following weeks as a strange blur. To her great credit, she somehow managed to function at her job without letting her standards slip.

James had eyed her with a great deal of scepticism as he heard rumours of the preparations. She seemed to have given in completely as Cameron and her family organised this and that, ordered, bought or made everything they considered necessary.

Her only real victory was managing to hold out over the dresses. She and her mother had spent a couple of Saturdays shopping in the West End stores for wedding finery.

Her dress was a dream. She had decided on a heavy, cream silk creation with a tightly-fitting bodice and long, straight skirt. The classic simplicity showed her slender figure to its best advantage and was free from clutter and frills. She would wear a simple coronet of fresh flowers in her hair and insisted she would have no veil.

Then Megan and her two bridesmaids spent a fun day choosing their outfits. Jane was fair and Lisa dark-haired, so they decided on a delicate peach shade in a similar style to the bridal gown. The bridesmaids, too, would wear flowers in their hair and the colours would be echoed in Megan's own bouquet.

At least now she felt she had made a positive contribution, however slight, to the proceedings.

Amidst all the rush, the time that Megan managed to spend alone with Cameron stood out like an oasis, and the only disquiet that she felt during those weeks was concerning Cameron's attitude to her work. He resented any time she gave to her job when they could have been together.

He had planned their honeymoon and refused to tell her anything about it.

'Come on, don't be so unfair. You must tell me where we're going,' she begged. 'How will I know what to pack?'

'I've told you. All you need are a couple of bikinis and some sun cream.'

'It's somewhere hot?'

'Maybe. Unless you've heard about an imminent heatwave in Scotland?'

He continued to tease her, throwing out unhelpful statements to mislead her.

A surprise was all very well but she wanted some idea of the sort of clothes she might need. She doubted many places would be prepared to allow her into the dining room, clad in just a bikini.

★ ★ ★

With just over a week to go before the wedding, Megan began to have serious doubts about the whole business.

'I wish we could simply elope and forget all this nonsense,' she grumbled to Lisa one morning. 'Honestly, is it worth it?'

'Really Megs, you don't know how lucky you are. It will be fabulous, just you wait.'

'I'm not even sure that Cameron and I are on the same planet,' she continued. 'He went into orbit when I said I was going to keep my flat. It will make a good bolt-hole when I have to work late. And Ewan can use it from time to time. It's not as if we needed the money I'd get if I sold it.'

Megan's face was looking rather pale and Lisa gave her fingers a comforting squeeze. She was certain that her friend's misgivings were no more than pre-wedding nerves and she tried to make light of them. 'It'll all be wonderful, just wait and see.'

'But I really don't know him. There

are so many things I have to discover about him. I don't even know if he likes cocoa.'

'Cocoa?' Lisa squeaked. 'What on earth does cocoa have to do with anything?'

'I binge on cocoa when I'm feeling really down. Jugs full of the stuff. But he doesn't know that. There are lots of things we don't know about each other. Silly little things as well as big important stuff.'

'Megan. Listen to me carefully. You love this guy. He obviously adores you. There are hundreds of little things you can spend the whole of your future learning about each other. If you knew everything all at once, you'd get bored with each other. You love each other. That's all that matters.'

Megan tried to keep her doubts to herself after this. She would soon be married to a wonderful man. He was handsome and kind and she was destined to be the happiest woman alive.

In two days time she was going home to spend the final few days remaining before the wedding with her parents. Tonight, she was going out with the office crowd. A sort of hen night but with the men there as well. Somehow, she had to pull herself out of this strange depression that she'd fallen into and be the life and soul of the party.

* * *

This proved to be easier than she expected. That evening, everyone was in a party mood, laughing and joking. When Megan looked round the room, she felt a warm glow of belonging, of being a part of something.

Cameron didn't understand her involvement in her job and, with his background, he probably didn't know the pleasure of being a member of a working team.

James called for silence and stood up to make the inevitable speech.

'From the very first day she walked

into the office, Megan has brought chaos, fun and an outstanding quality of work into our lives. She has never ceased to surprise us with her off-beat attitude and spontaneous approach to life.' He paused as her colleagues murmured their agreement. 'But the speed with which she met her man and organised a wedding is spectacular. I do believe she is a one-off. The world could never cope with more than one Megan Belmore!' He paused again as everyone laughed, then he turned to Megan with a smile. 'Seriously, love, we all wish you every happiness and hope you will accept this gift from us all as a token of our love. We shall really miss you. To Megan and Cameron,' he concluded, raising his glass.

'To Megan and Cameron,' chorused her friends and colleagues. 'Speech!' they all shouted.

Blushing, she rose to her feet.

'Thank you all. Everything's happened so quickly, I can hardly believe it. Thank you for the gift and I shall look forward to seeing everyone at the wedding.'

Feeling as if she might burst into tears at any moment, she sat down quickly. 'I guess it's OK to open it now?' she asked, looking at the beautifully wrapped gift and tugging at the ribbons.

It was an elaborately engraved silver tray.

'It's lovely,' she said. 'I shall treasure it. Thank you all.'

As she travelled home in a taxi, she felt suddenly bereft. It was the end of one era and the beginning of the next — because she had finally given in to Cameron's badgering and had handed in her notice.

It had seemed the easiest thing to do. James had promised her some freelance work but already she was missing the thought of working full-time. And in a few days she would no longer be Megan Belmore but Megan Marshall. Was she doing the right thing? A new name, a new life. She wondered how Cameron would feel if she used her old name for her byline in her future articles.

★ ★ ★

There were three days to go. It seemed that Mona was always on the phone to either Jane or Cameron. Cameron had employed a team of gardeners to get the grounds looking their best and a troop of decorators had ensured that the inside of the house was also perfect.

Megan had not seen her future husband for two days and, apart from a rather formal dinner party the following evening, she wouldn't see him again until the wedding.

She complained to her mother that she had nothing to do.

'Make the most of it,' Mona had told her before rushing away to make yet another of her endless phone calls.

'Fancy a drink down at the pub, later?' Ewan suggested when he came home from work.

'Wonderful. Just what I need,' she

replied gratefully.

The brother and sister went out as soon as they'd finished their evening meal and once she had relaxed a little, Ewan took Megan's hand.

'What's up, Megs?' he asked. 'And don't say nothing because I know you too well.'

Fighting back tears, she poured out all her doubts and fears and finally said miserably, 'There's no-one I can tell. No-one I can talk to. Everyone said I was rushing into something I couldn't handle. I daren't admit they were right. Ewan, I don't think I can go through with it.'

'If you're serious, then we'll talk to Mum when we get home. She'll understand. My diagnosis is pre-wedding nerves. You love the guy, don't you?'

'Of course I do. I'm just a bit scared of such a massive commitment.'

'You don't have to go through with it if you don't want to,' he said softly.

'Don't I?'

'Not if you have serious doubts,' he

assured her. 'I'll stand by you if you want to change your mind. Better now than later.'

But when they returned home and Ewan explained to their mother that Megan was having second thoughts, Mona exploded.

'You ungrateful girl,' she almost shouted. 'After everything that has been done for you. How dare you tell me at so late a stage? I tried to warn you but, oh no, you were certain that Cameron was the man for you. You loved him and wanted to be married as soon as possible. No, Megan. I'm not even going to listen to this nonsense. Cameron and your father have spent a small fortune on this wedding. Think how it would look to all the people we've invited. There are nearly two hundred guests coming on Friday. The marquee is already in place, and all the presents. No, Megan. It's too late.'

White with fury, Megan turned and went out of the room. She lay on her bed and sobbed herself to sleep.

Next morning, her mother brought her a cup of tea in bed. 'Feeling better, dear? Pre-wedding nerves, that's all that's wrong with you. It happens to everyone.'

Later that morning, Megan went out for a walk with the family dog, an ancient spaniel. She walked up the hill behind her parents' house, and sat on the grass with him, fondling his soft ears.

'Dear old Benson. You have the easy life.'

He wagged his little tail and flopped down, panting.

She sat staring at the view over the rolling countryside, glad of the peace, and thought of going away where no-one could find her.

Then she sighed heavily as she saw someone walking up the path towards her. The last thing she wanted was company.

The man who was approaching her

was tall and athletic in his movements. His dark head was held high. It was Cameron.

He sat down beside her on the grass.

'I hope I'm not intruding,' he apologised, 'but it's been so long since we last met that I was desperate to see you.'

'How on earth did you know where to find me?' she asked.

'Ewan. He said you often came up here to think.'

'Oh? And when were you speaking to Ewan?'

'He called me this morning. Thought it would be a good idea for us to talk.'

Suddenly, Cameron's confident manner disappeared.

'Have you changed your mind? Don't you love me after all?' he asked.

'Oh, Cameron, I'm sure that I love you, but I feel like a puppet. Everyone is frantically busy organising everything and I feel like some inanimate object in the middle. What a fuss you're all making. It gets crazier by the second.

No-one lets me do anything. I wish I'd stayed at work.'

He put a comforting arm round her.

'Don't turn me away. I couldn't bear it. I love you, Megan. I shall be so proud to have you as my wife.'

He kissed her gently on the cheek. Then he put a finger under her chin and turned her towards him, placed his lips on hers.

The dog stood up and shook himself.

'Not in front of the dog.' She smiled, releasing herself from his arms.

'I just wanted to remind you how much I love you.'

'I know. And I love you, too. Don't worry. I've just got pre-wedding nerves. Let's take Benson back and you can buy me lunch at the pub. Or I'll buy lunch for you. Just to prove I'm an independent woman.'

'Now there's an offer I can't refuse. Your mother won't mind?'

'Who cares? Come on. Let's go,' she ordered and leapt to her feet.

Benson gave a short bark, glad to be

on the move again.

As soon as Megan returned home, her mother pounced upon her.

'Where on earth have you been, you naughty girl?' she asked. 'We've been worried sick. It's time to get ready for the rehearsal. Now, what time are we collecting your friend from the station, and have you got everything ready to go straight on to the dinner? And where are your father and Ewan?'

Mona rushed off and Megan sighed.

* * *

When she awoke on her wedding day, Megan could hear the steady dripping of water. She looked out of her window and saw heavy grey clouds everywhere and the rain pouring down. Mona knocked on the door and came in carrying a tray of breakfast.

'Oh, you're up!' she said sounding very disappointed.

'I just got up to look at the weather. I can easy get back into bed. Isn't it awful out there? My cream shoes will be mud-coloured before I've walked across to the marquee.'

'The forecast says it will get better later. Don't worry. And there's a proper floor in the marquee.'

Mona tried to comfort her daughter but she herself was desperately disappointed. All their plans relied on the sun shining and the photographs would have been so much better taken outside.

'Maybe it's an omen,' Megan suggested cynically.

'I won't have you talking like that. Now, enjoy your breakfast before it goes cold. The hairdresser is coming at ten.'

★ ★ ★

The wedding went without a hitch, but Megan felt she was playing a part in some theatrical production. Her mother's endless lists, pinned all around the house, ensured that she was in the right places at the right times. Everything was arranged to the last detail and she moved through the orchestrated events like an actor playing her role.

She spoke to dozens of people she had never met before and accepted congratulations from friends and relations she had not seen since she was a child.

Cameron seemed to have no actual family, but made up his share of the guest list with business colleagues and friends. The best man was the same friend who had proposed the toast at their engagement party. He made a witty speech and was applauded loudly. The excitement in the air was infectious and even the rain stopped.

'When do you think we can escape?' Cameron whispered to Megan as evening fell.

'You'd better ask my mother what point we've reached in the master plan. She's had everything timed to the last second. What is it? 6.03? I think that means it's time to pick up a plate and eat fifty grams of wedding cake. No more. No less.'

'You do exaggerate. Everything's gone very smoothly. Poor woman. She looks as if she's on her knees. Come on, let's make our farewells. It's time I had my wife to myself.'

He leaned over to kiss her, an event not missed by the man with the video camera who seemed to have been at their elbows for the entire day. A few of the nearby guests applauded.

'Shall I help you to change into your going away outfit?' asked Lisa, whose bridesmaid's role was almost over. 'I think that's what I'm supposed to do, isn't it? Whoops. Too much champagne,' she said as she tottered to her feet, stumbling against Cameron's arm. 'Lovely man, your husband, Megan. Such a gentleman.'

'I think you're the one needing *my* help.' Megan laughed.

★ ★ ★

It was almost another hour before they could get away. Cameron had booked a hotel for the night so that they could make an early start for the airport the next morning.

Their destination was still a secret and, as instructed, Megan had packed two bikinis and a tube of sun-screen. She had also added a few light, summery clothes, anticipating a holiday somewhere exotic and hot.

'Well, Mrs Marshall, how does it feel to be a married woman at last?' Cameron was pouring champagne from a bottle left in their hotel suite. He handed it to her. 'You can enjoy a drink now it's all over. Personally, I have drunk enough orange juice to last me a lifetime.'

'Do you know what I want at this moment?' she said. 'I'd kill for a sandwich. I don't seem to have had time to eat. Every time I got close to that delicious looking buffet, someone rushed up and gave me a hug or a kiss. I'd even go for that fifty grams of wedding cake.'

'I've married a glutton,' he moaned.

'Here I am, on my wedding night and she wants a sandwich. What did I do wrong?'

She giggled at his sad expression and kissed him.

'Sorry, darling. I'll starve, don't worry. What are you doing?' she asked as he crossed the room.

'Looking for the room service menu. I'm ordering you a sandwich. Ham, cheese or chicken?'

'One of each, please. Then there'll still be some left for me after you've eaten your share.'

Honeymoon Days

The unfamiliar shrieking of the hotel telephone woke them just before eight o'clock the next morning.

'Come on. We'll have to hurry,' he told her. 'Breakfast's on its way. I've ordered room service to save us the bother of going down to the dining-room. Put something comfortable on. We've a lot of travelling to do over the next couple of days.'

'Where on earth are we going?' she asked. 'Nowhere takes that long to get to.'

'Indonesia.'

Megan frowned. For a moment, she couldn't even think where it was.

'We arrive in Singapore tomorrow morning and then it's a few hours to Indonesia. It will probably take most of the next day to reach our final destination.'

'You are being deliberately evasive,' she grumbled. 'Exactly where is this final destination?'

'Ever heard of Bali?' he asked.

'Bali?' she squeaked. 'You mean we're actually going to Bali? Wow!'

'I hoped you'd be pleased. Now, get dressed and open the door to the waiter, while I shower. I promise you, Bali will be worth the long journey when we finally get there.'

Megan looked at her new husband, loving him more every moment.

★ ★ ★

It was dark when they finally reached their hotel in Bali after a journey that seemed to have gone on forever. It was warm and humid and the air was filled with the humming of tropical night creatures. Tiny lanterns lit the pathways and exotic flowers bloomed everywhere. Even in the pitch darkness, it was everything Megan had dreamed of.

'Oh, Cameron,' she whispered. 'Isn't

this wonderful?'

She held his arm and snuggled close to him as they stood on their balcony overlooking the beach. The moon cast a silvery light over everything as it shone from a navy-blue sky dotted with silver stars. They could see palms silhouetted against white sands and an almost luminous line of pale beach fringing the dark sea.

'I'm glad you thought it worth the trip.'

'It is truly paradise,' she replied.

★ ★ ★

The following days were spent lazing round the glorious swimming pool, eating wonderful food. Several afternoons, they took the tourist trips out to see the local villages. As darkness fell so suddenly in the tropics, the drama of traditional dances was enhanced by the light of torches and fires.

One night, as they were eating barbecued lobster in the beach-side restaurant, Cameron became quiet. He took her hand and spoke seriously.

'You are enjoying yourself, aren't you?'

'Do you need to ask?' she said softly. 'This has been a truly wonderful honeymoon, so far. And we still have another two weeks here, haven't we?'

'Err . . . well, no. I hope you don't mind but we're going to move on.'

She looked surprised.

'We're flying to Sydney, the day after tomorrow,' he told her.

'Australia? Oh, Cameron, you're amazing. I can't believe it.' The excitement in her voice seemed to be a relief to him.

'I was worried that you might not want to leave Bali. But Sydney is lovely and you'll enjoy the shopping and the sights there. You'll be able to buy any extra clothes you need.'

'Good job I did pack a bit more than a bikini,' she said, laughing.

'To make up for leaving Bali, I've arranged a special day out for us tomorrow. I've hired a boat and a local diver. We're going snorkelling over the coral reef.'

'Sounds great, but I'm not the world's greatest swimmer, you know.'

He reassured her that that would be no problem. The diver would show them what to do and he would be there with them, all the time.

When their meal was over, they walked hand in hand along the beach before going to bed.

★ ★ ★

Despite her qualms, the snorkelling expedition turned into another wonderful and memorable day. She was given an old inner tube to float in so that she could look down into the water in safety.

'Once you can do that happily, we'll take away the tube and you can go solo,' said Wattra, their guide.

His broad grin was infectious and his liquid brown eyes held a glint of wickedness that suggested he was always fun to be with. He leapt over the side of the boat and went down into the water until he was out of sight.

Cameron, complete with snorkel, fins and mask, dived in after him. Megan was more cautious and let herself over the side gently and held on to her floating tube. Then she put on the mask and lowered her face into the sea.

From the surface of the shining water, there was nothing much to see but as soon as she could look beneath, she saw a world that left her breathless.

The most brilliantly coloured fish were darting everywhere and coral grew like forests of exotic trees. She gasped with delight as she came up for air.

Determinedly, she fitted the snorkel into her mouth and soon got the hang of it. When they all finally climbed back into the boat, she was almost speechless with joy.

'The fish are so tame,' she said. 'They swim really close to you. And the colours. I've never seen anything like them.'

Wattra laughed, showing rows of the whitest teeth.

'Now, I take you for barbecue. Red mullet, lobster, whatever you want.'

He hauled up a canopy to shade them from the midday sun, and Cameron and Megan sat side by side, watching the waves scud by the little boat.

Cameron reached into their bag and produced the sun-screen. He rubbed some into Megan's shoulders, placing a light silk shirt over her.

'You mustn't burn. With your colouring, you are very vulnerable.' He leaned over and kissed her. 'Can't have my one and only wife rivalling the lobsters, can I?'

★　★　★

All too soon, the day was over, and while they ate their last dinner in Bali, they talked about the things they had seen and done there.

'I hope you're not too disappointed

to be leaving earlier than planned,' Cameron said, looking troubled.

'Just a little sad, but I'd feel that, even if we'd been here for months. Do you remember that day we drove through the centre of the island and stopped to look at rice terraces? From nowhere, that little group of children appeared.'

Cameron smiled indulgently.

'We'll come back one day. With our own children, perhaps.'

'Frightening thought,' she remarked.

He stared at her for a moment but said nothing.

* * *

The flight to Sydney was relatively easy, and Megan was thrilled to see so many sights she recognised as they flew over the city. The whole panorama of deep-blue sea with white boats dotted everywhere, the magnificent opera house, and the famous bridge that represents Sydney to so many people, seemed so familiar.

She squeaked with excitement and Cameron laughed, caught up in her enthusiasm.

'We're taking a trip round the harbour tomorrow. I have several acquaintances who live here. Maxie and Geoff run a boat charter business and we'll be meeting them tomorrow. It isn't the best time of year — it can be cool towards the outer harbour.'

'So much for the bikini and sun-cream,' she teased.

'Look, it's only three o'clock,' he told her after they'd arrived at their hotel. 'The shops will be open for some time. Why don't you go and buy yourself a couple of warmer sweaters, jeans, that sort of thing? There are taxis outside the hotel.'

He handed her a roll of notes and some loose dollars for her fares.

'What are you going to do?' she asked, disappointed that he didn't want to go with her her.

'I have a few calls to make. I need to see various people while we are here.

You'll be meeting some of them tomorrow and then we're invited to dinner with Maxie and Geoff afterwards.'

Megan sensed the honeymoon was nearly over. Their intimate little dinners had come to an end and something new was beginning. With the ghost of a sigh, she took the money he was holding out and left the room.

She hated taking handouts all the time but with no Australian currency of her own, she had little choice.

★　★　★

Outside in the streets, there was a constant flow of people. Somehow, even in the Australian winter, the town seemed more casual than London.

She wandered around, taking care not to get lost, looking into shops that could have been transported from any town anywhere. She supposed that shopping was shopping wherever you were in the western world.

When she went back to the hotel, Cameron wasn't in and she had to go to the desk to ask for the key, panicking for a moment when they said there was no-one by the name of Belmore staying there. Then, blushing madly, she remembered. The receptionist gave a knowing smile and handed her the key.

'Takes a bit of getting used to, doesn't it?'

'About the next hundred years I expect,' she said with a grin.

'Congratulations, Mrs Marshall. I hope you'll be very happy. We've known Mr Marshall for many years.'

'He's stayed here often then, has he?' she asked with some surprise.

'Yes, of course.' The woman looked uncomfortable, as if she had been less than discreet.

Megan returned to their room and glanced round. No note to say where her husband had gone. She gave a shrug and ran a bath, lying back, relaxed and enjoying a wallow.

'Hi, darling,' came Cameron's voice

through the door. She gave a start, realising that she'd almost dozed off.

'Sorry. I had to go out to see someone about a business deal,' he told her as he came into the bathroom. 'You look comfortable. Enjoy your shopping? Did you find what you needed?'

* * *

'You didn't tell me you'd stayed here before,' Megan said as they finished their coffee after dinner.

'Didn't I? It didn't seem important. Is it?'

'I just wish you'd said. I realised you must have been to Australia before but the receptionist mentioned that you stayed here regularly and I . . . well, I felt a little foolish. So, tell me about tomorrow. What are our plans?' she said as brightly as she could.

'Well, after breakfast, Maxie and Geoff are coming to collect us to take us around the harbour and out past some of the islands in their boat.'

'Sounds great,' Megan said enthusiastically. 'Do you have any other work things to do while we're here?'

'Just a meeting or two while you shop and spend a small fortune. The Australian share of the wine market is growing. I want to get exclusive contracts with some of the vineyards so I need to make a few trips out of the city to visit a couple of growers. That way, I can make sure I do the best deals. You can stay here or come with me, although I expect it will be pretty boring talk. The trouble with Australia is that it's so huge. I shall fly to a couple of places from here and then we'll move on to South Australia.'

★ ★ ★

Maxie and Geoff proved to be an interesting couple and Megan was totally captivated by the magnificent sights that Sydney had to offer.

The large boat cruised round the spectacular harbour while they all relaxed on the deck. Geoff and Cameron disappeared for a short time to discuss some business.

'We're very fond of Cameron,' Maxie told Megan. 'And we're so delighted he's found you. He's had a tough time in the past and deserves a little happiness. Now, tell me all about yourself. I want to know how you met and how long you've known each other.'

Megan repeated her tale. She was wondering what Maxie could have meant by a tough time.

Obviously there was something in Cameron's past that he hadn't told her about, unless Maxie was simply referring to the untimely death of his parents.

She relaxed, allowing herself to make the most of this wonderful trip. Her married life was going to be exciting, interesting and filled with Cameron's love. She was indeed, a very lucky lady.

★ ★ ★

After eating an excellent lunch, down in the luxurious cabin, Megan went up on deck for some fresh air. The wind was rising and she shivered in the sudden chill.

She gazed around, trying to imprint every detail on her mind. Her parents would be so thrilled to hear about it.

She felt a momentary pang of homesickness for her family.

Cameron appeared and came to stand behind her, putting his arm on her shoulder.

'Penny for them?' he said at last.

'I was just thinking about my parents and Ewan. They'll never believe all this.'

'Feeling homesick?' he asked.

'Not really homesick. Can you be people sick?'

'You're not regretting it, are you? Marrying me, I mean?'

His eyes looked troubled.

'Of course not. No, as you say, it's just a touch of nostalgia. I love you, Cameron.'

Then Maxie and Geoff appeared on

deck and began making plans for several more outings together, suggesting places to visit. They offered to lend their friends a car for the rest of their stay, allowing them to get around more easily.

★ ★ ★

During the days that followed, Cameron and Megan visited various tourist attractions, attended a concert in the magnificent opera house, and had a couple of meals with their new friends.

For Megan, one of the most special days was a drive out to the Blue Mountains. The wild, unspoilt land stretched forever. It was the first real wilderness she had seen and the sheer extent of it left her feeling breathless.

'Makes you realise just how small we are,' she murmured. 'I've never been anywhere quite like this before.'

'There is nowhere else quite like this. But you have seen only the tiniest part of this country so far. We're moving on soon. I'm taking you to see some of the wine producing regions later. Give you a better idea of what Australia is all about. I'm flying out to the Hunter Valley tomorrow. It will be a very long day but I should be back late in the evening.'

She felt a little sad that this was all happening during their honeymoon but she didn't complain. After all, her husband's wealth was the result of sheer hard work.

★ ★ ★

'If this isn't enough money for what you want, just use your own credit cards,' Cameron said, handing her a large bundle of notes. 'I'll settle all your bills from now on, so don't worry about how much you spend. Oh, and Maxie is going to give you a call to see if you want any company.'

It was only six-thirty in the morning but Cameron's long journey meant an early start for him.

Megan lay in bed, watching him get ready.

'How do I look?' he asked.

'Much too smart for a honeymoon,' she said without thinking.

'I'm sorry,' he said, 'but I do have a business to look after. I'll see you later.'

She couldn't help feeling just a little piqued that this honeymoon had obviously been planned from the beginning to fit in with Cameron's business meetings. Maybe this was the reason for his insistence on rushing ahead with the wedding.

She stretched and rolled over. A whole day spent shopping would be too much, even for her. Besides, she had plenty of clothes now and enough souvenirs to stock several shops.

She wrote a postcard home to her parents and picked up a guide book, leafing through it for inspiration,

Then Maxie rang, suggesting they should visit some of the markets and Megan accepted her invitation gratefully.

'Right,' Maxie said as they finished lunch. 'Are you ready to set off again? There's an interesting antiques market near here. The sort of flea market where you pay the earth for utter rubbish but sometimes manage to find a bargain. By the way, what are you planning to do this evening? Geoff and I are going to our favourite jazz club. They do fairly simple, basic food but it's fun. You're welcome to join us. I gather Cameron won't be back until pretty late. Do say you'll come. It will do you good to have an evening out. You don't want him to think you are always sitting at home waiting for him.'

'You're right. And it sounds like fun. Thanks very much. I'd love to join you.'

★ ★ ★

There was a sense of the Old Colonial about the jazz club. The décor was deliberately downmarket with benches and rough wooden tables.

The band were a very competent group, noisy but perfect for their surroundings.

Geoff, Maxie and Megan ate enormous steak sandwiches and bowls of fries with their fingers, and drank beer from cans. There was no opportunity for conversation but there was plenty of laughter. It was after eleven before Geoff suggested they might leave.

Back at her hotel, Megan found Cameron lying on their bed, his head resting on his arms. He lifted himself on to one elbow and looked at her.

'You're back before me,' she said in surprise.

'Obviously. Where on earth have you been? I was frantic. Reception had no idea where you were. Said you'd gone out this morning with a friend but they hadn't seen you again. No-one could shop for this long.'

His voice was shaking with suppressed anger and there was no sign of his usual smile.

Megan stared in surprise. She was unable to speak for a moment. Then she drew in her breath and said, 'Maxie and Geoff invited me out to a jazz club they know. I had supper with them. I enjoyed myself.'

'But you hate jazz,' Cameron retorted.

'No, I don't. It isn't my favourite music but I certainly don't hate it. You must be confusing me with someone else.'

'I certainly hate jazz,' he snapped.

'Then it's a good job I went without you. Have you eaten?'

'I was hoping to share dinner with my wife.'

'So you haven't eaten?'

'I ate a little bit of smoked salmon on the flight. A vol au vent or two. Nothing you could call dinner.'

'And was it a good trip?'

'Spoilt only by my lack of welcome home, yes, I suppose it was.'

'You're being petty, Cameron. I had no idea when you'd be back and it was a long day. They are your friends and

149

they were only trying to look after me. Perhaps you'd like something to eat now? Shall I phone for something?'

'Don't bother. I'm too tired now. I'm going to bed.'

Megan brushed her teeth and got in beside him. He was either fast asleep or feigning it. She gave a sigh and quickly fell asleep herself.

★　★　★

Next day at breakfast, he made no mention of the previous evening. This was their last day in Sydney. They were flying to Victoria that afternoon.

The next few days became a blur and, although she adored seeing all the new places, she could scarcely remember where they had been and all the people they had met. When she counted the days, she realised they were close to the end of their trip.

'Yes, darling,' Cameron confirmed. 'We fly home in two days. I hope this has been a honeymoon you will remember.'

'It's been great,' she said, her voice lacking enthusiasm.

'You don't sound as if you mean that, not one hundred per cent.'

'Oh, but I do. I just feel slightly confused, I suppose. I wasn't prepared for quite so much travelling around.'

'I had to show you off to all my friends. I'm very proud of my new wife. I'm sorry if you're disappointed.'

'Of course I'm not. Please don't think that I haven't enjoyed myself.'

'Come on, then. We're lunching with some of my oldest and dearest friends.'

And so Megan faced yet another set of his *oldest* and *dearest* friends.

'I'm going to have to buy another suitcase,' she grumbled as she packed, later that day. Her small bag had long ago ceased to be sufficient as she bought more and more clothes and souvenirs but, so far, she had managed to stuff the extra things in various holdalls.

Cameron reached into his pocket and handed over yet another bundle of dollars.

'Cameron, I don't want endless handouts. If I'd known where we were going, I could have brought what I needed in the first place.'

'Well, in that case I'd better tell you where we're going next. We're stopping over in Singapore for a couple of days, to give you a chance to do some shopping in that wonderful city.'

He looked so pleased with his surprise that she didn't have the heart to tell him that if she never saw a shop again it would be too soon. She simply smiled and went out to buy another suitcase.

★　★　★

The bustle of Singapore was yet another new experience. They had spent the morning wandering around, bewildered by the huge array of goods and the bargain prices. This was like shopping nowhere else in the world.

But, for Megan, the sight of so many shopping malls was too much.

'Let's go somewhere silly this afternoon,' she begged. 'The zoo or one of the other touristy places I saw on the brochures at the hotel.'

Time alone with Cameron was just what she needed. They wandered around the zoo looking at the animals, and she realised that this was a new experience for him. He'd missed out on so many childhood things and this was his first ever visit to a zoo.

'I can't believe it.' Megan laughed. 'Didn't you ever have birthday treats? Ewan and I always chose the zoo for birthday outings. Mum and Dad used to get thoroughly sick of it! Ewan graduated to the Science Museum after a while, and I grew to like the Planetarium and Madame Tussauds but only if it was too wet for the zoo.'

Cameron had visited none of the places she mentioned and she made a resolution to take him to them as soon as she could.

'You may be on speaking terms with the rest of the world,' she said, 'but you have a lot to catch up on in the UK.'

'We shall be able to begin my education quite soon,' Cameron observed. 'We shall be back there tomorrow. The beginning of the rest of our lives.'

'The real beginning of our life together,' she said softly.

Married Life

Jane welcomed the newly-weds home. Knowing they would be feeling jet-lagged, she had organised a simple meal and then left them alone while she went out for the evening. Megan was grateful. She liked Jane enormously but she knew that living with a third person was going to be difficult.

Apart from Jane, who had her own rooms in the house, there was a couple who lived in a cottage in the grounds. Mrs Baines came in every day to organise the cleaning and do the cooking, while Mr Baines looked after the garden.

'Don't you want to phone your parents?' Cameron suggested. 'Let them know we're safely back?'

'I think I'll wait till tomorrow. They'll want to chat and I feel exhausted. I could sleep for hours.'

Once they had been back home for a few days, Megan realised that the capable Mrs Baines had everything to do with running the house under control and she had very little to do with her time.

She had called her parents on her first day back from honeymoon and had promised to go over to see them as soon as she could. But Cameron had gone off in his car and Jane was also working away from home, so Megan had no transport. She mooched around, thinking that the honeymoon was well and truly over.

Thoroughly bored, she phoned her old workplace. She missed her friends and the pressure of having deadlines to meet. But when she was finally put through to the newsroom, everyone was frantically busy. Even Lisa couldn't spare any time to talk but promised they would meet soon for a gossip.

Next, Megan phoned her mother but she was out.

'If this is the start of my new life,' she muttered, 'I'm not impressed.'

There must be something to occupy her. When Cameron came back that evening, she was determined to talk it through with him.

'But you don't need to work,' he said predictably. 'Enjoy life. Maybe we should start our family. We've no reason to wait. I'd like to have children before I reach thirty-five, otherwise I'll be too old to play football with them or take them to your beloved zoo.'

'But I'm not ready to have children yet,' Megan said, her eyes wide with fear.

'Nonsense. If everyone waited till they were ready, we'd never have a future generation. This is the perfect time for us to have a family. I love you so much, Megan.'

'Oh, Cameron. I'm truly not ready for this. I'm not ready for the responsibility of children. A couple of months ago, we'd scarcely met. We need time together as a couple before we start a family. Please, Cameron, listen to what I'm saying.'

'I have an early start,' he said shortly.

★　★　★

That night, Megan lay awake beside her husband. Towards dawn, she must have drifted off, because she didn't wake when he got up, dressed and left for his office.

Her first priority that day was to find something to occupy herself. She had some phone calls to make. She knew her plans would not please Cameron but what she had to do was for her own good. She would be delighted to have Cameron's babies, but when she was ready, and not without discussing the implications thoroughly first.

The Bucks Guardian was a much smaller concern than her previous paper. Its target audience lived outside London and their requirements were different. She looked at back copies of the paper. When she felt satisfied that she knew what it was all about, she telephone the editor to ask if he would see her.

She put together some samples of her work and prepared thoroughly for an informal interview the following day.

She also made an appointment to see the local doctor.

She didn't intend to tell Cameron anything about all this until she knew she might have at least the offer of some sort of job.

That evening he was late returning home.

'I have to go to London again, tomorrow,' he grumbled. 'I was hoping we could do something together but that will have to wait. How about you come with me and we can meet up later? You've been complaining about being bored. You might like to check that your flat is OK. You should consider selling it. It's unlikely you'll ever use it again. How about seeing an estate agent tomorrow? I can give you a couple of names. Then we could meet up when I've finished with my business and go to a theatre or something. What do you say?'

Megan gulped. What could she say? She had a job interview and an appointment to see the doctor. Neither of these activities was going to please Cameron.

'Nice idea, darling, but I have made other plans for tomorrow.'

'Oh, really? That's good. What are you doing?'

Having no idea what to say, she began, 'I'm planning to see Mum and an old friend. I was going to ask if I could borrow your car, otherwise I'll have to get a taxi.'

'We must see about getting you a little runabout. It's ridiculous for you to be without transport out here. I'm sorry I didn't think of it before. Go down to the local dealer in the morning and see what he's got. If there's something you fancy, take it out on a test drive when you go to see your mother.'

'You mean to say that the garage owner would entrust a car to a complete stranger for the day?'

'He's not exactly a stranger. He knows me well. I'll call him and set it up.'

★   ★   ★

As promised, Cameron phoned the garage the next morning before he left for London.

'He thinks he's got just the thing for you. It isn't new but he says it's a nice car. It's low mileage and in good condition. You can have it if it's what you want. Go and look. If you call him, he'll come out to pick you up.'

'Oh, Cameron. Thanks so much, but I plan to buy this car for myself.'

'Whatever you like. But can you afford it? Must get off now.'

Megan stood chewing her nails. The truth was, she couldn't really afford a car, not unless she sold the flat. She could try out the car, as arranged, and discuss it later with Cameron. She would also take the chance to discuss it and a hundred and one other things with her mother. She dialled her old home number and her mother answered.

'Hello, Mum. Can I come over to see you later today? Are you busy?'

'Megan, it's lovely to hear from you. I'd love to see you. Seems strange that you're not working. I haven't got used to the idea yet. Perhaps we shall see a bit more of you now.'

Megan told her mother that she'd arrive for lunch sometime after one o'clock. That should give her plenty time for her plans.

The car dealer arrived with the car and she drove it back to the garage with him. It was perfect.

'You take it out for the day, Mrs Marshall. Then, if you like it, your husband says he'll settle up later.'

She went back home first, to collect her portfolio of work to take with her to her interview, and to change. She dressed in a simple suit, hoping to look smart and businesslike. Not quite the outfit she might have chosen for visiting her mother but that couldn't be helped. Her first call, however, was to the doctor's surgery.

* * *

The editor of The Bucks Guardian was nothing like her previous boss, James. He was older for a start and seemed to have a very much more laid-back approach to the local news.

'We don't have a full-time vacancy at the moment, but we are looking for a couple of part-timers. It won't be regular hours. And you wouldn't be getting the big time stuff you're used to. You'd be covering the local produce show and amateur opera — that sort of thing. But there are times when everything happens at once and we just can't cover it all. Are you interested?'

'I'd be very happy with part-time. I'm hoping to do some freelance stuff for my old paper. You wouldn't have any objection to that, would you?'

He frowned slightly.

'Depends on the subject matter. If it was something that would be of interest to our readers then we'd have first call on you.'

Megan nodded her agreement. And surely if she was only working part-time, Cameron could have no objections.

'Right then,' Mr Henderson concluded, 'we'll be in touch. Glad to have you on board. We'll sort out a contract and I'll call you when I've got an event for you to cover.'

'I'll look forward to that,' Megan said, grinning. It was a start and she felt better already. She was regaining control of her life. Much as she adored Cameron, she needed some independence. She set out for her parents' home.

'Darling! You look marvellous!' Mona flung her arms round her daughter. 'Come on in. I want to hear all your news. Your father was coming home for lunch so that he could see you, too, but something came up.'

She hugged her daughter, her face wreathed in smiles of happiness.

'Everything is still wonderful, isn't it, love?' Mona asked anxiously.

'Of course it is. I love Cameron like crazy. He's a dream of a man and I'm very lucky.'

'It sounds as if there's a but coming.'

'We don't entirely see eye to eye about my working life. And families. He seems determined we should start a family almost immediately.'

Megan's voice cracked slightly as she tried to hold back the unexpected tears that burned.

'You'd do well to wait a while. Give yourselves time to get to know each other.'

Megan nodded.

'How's Dad?' she asked, changing the subject. 'Is he taking things more easily? Ewan must be a help.'

'Oh, he certainly is. If only your father would think about retiring. But you know him. Thinks the world will fall apart if he takes a morning off.'

The two talked on — pausing for several cups of tea and coffee — until late.

'Heavens, I must get back,' Megan exclaimed. 'Cameron will think I've deserted him. It's been lovely to chat. I can't remember when we last sat like this all afternoon.'

'Golly, I can. After you thought you'd failed your A levels,' Mona said with a laugh. 'You've grown up, Megan.'

They hugged; a new understanding and equality between them. Megan knew her mother would become her new confidante. She had grown up. It was time to get on with the serious business of adult life.

* * *

'How was your day?' she asked Cameron when she arrived back.

'Not bad. A very busy day and it was all a bit of a rush, but I managed to do everything. How did you get on with the car?'

'It's gorgeous and goes really well. Just what I wanted,' she said with enthusiasm. 'But I forgot to ask the price. Is it very expensive?'

He named a figure that made her gasp slightly. She had never had anything much to do with cars and the sum he mentioned sounded like a fortune. There was no way she could afford that much money.

'I take it you'll accept my offer of a gift?' he said, smiling.

Independence was too expensive!

'If you're sure,' she said doubtfully. 'It is a lot more than I can afford. But I will pay you back, I promise.'

He gave a shrug.

They swapped tales of their separate days but Megan knew she was holding back, telling him nothing of her visit to the local newspaper or doctor. Already she was keeping secrets. She thought about Simone's words after they had announced their engagement. '*You organise their lives the way you want to.*' Megan understood her words now. Once Cameron had accepted that they were going to have to wait for a while before starting a family, he would be more understanding and maybe more tolerant of her need to work.

★ ★ ★

Jane seemed to spend a lot of time away from home, giving them space. Cameron continued his trips to London several times a week. Megan visited her mother, went shopping and pottered round the house and garden.

She still felt bored with so little to do.

Someone else did the housework, looked after the garden and did the cooking.

When she thought she'd go mad with inactivity, the editor of the local paper telephoned, at last. He had some stories for her to follow up. This was her chance. She was delighted at the prospect of doing something she enjoyed and could do well. She planned to tell Cameron about the job when they were having dinner. He couldn't object to her working a few days a week.

'I've got some good news,' she began enthusiastically, when they were seated at the dining table.

'Oh, darling! I'm so thrilled! You've made me the proudest man in the world. Whoops . . . no more wine for you, I'm afraid,' he said with a grin. 'Tell you what, I'll give it up as well. At home, anyhow.'

'Cameron, what are you talking about?'

'A baby. You said you were going to have a baby.'

'No, I didn't. I said I had some good news.' Megan felt irritated. It was obvious that there was only one piece of news he wanted to hear but he would have a long wait. His handsome face fell.

'Go on then. What's your news?' he said with mock cheerfulness.

'I've got a job. Just part-time on the local paper.'

Cameron's face grew angry. His eyes darkened and took on a steely look. His jaw tightened.

'You know how you're always telling me you want me to be happy? Well, this makes me happy. Aren't you going to congratulate me?'

He said nothing but continued to glare at her, almost in disbelief. Finally, he folded his napkin and got up from the table.

'Cameron? Say something,' she begged. 'Don't you want any pudding?'

'You know how I feel about you working. I thought we'd been through this before the wedding. If you'd wanted to work, you should have stayed with your old job, not joined some local rag with a zero circulation.'

'You're being ridiculous,' Megan said, her temper flaring. 'I'm bored with spending my days aimlessly wandering round here. There's a gardener who comes in to do the garden. Mrs Baines does all the cooking and cleaning and if I venture into the kitchen, she chases me out. So what am I supposed to do? Even your sister is working and motivated.'

'I've paid a generous allowance into your account. You don't need the money. I'm a highly successful businessman. I don't want my wife going out to work every day.'

'But it's about more than the money. My work is important. I think you're being unreasonable.'

'I don't see what's unreasonable about wanting a family. In fact, I don't know why you're not pregnant yet. Perhaps there's something wrong with one of us. Maybe we should see a specialist. I'll look into it.'

He walked over to the window so she couldn't see his expression of fear.

'Cameron,' Megan said with a deadly calm. 'I don't want to sit around the house all day. I intend to follow my career. I am thrilled to have this job, however small and insignificant. I need something stimulating to occupy me.'

'I'm sorry, but surely I'm working hard enough for two.'

'I know that, Cameron. But I need to work for me. I am bored. Unfulfilled. Please try to understand. How would you feel if your work was suddenly taken away? Please give me a chance and don't be like one of those Victorian husbands insisting on the little wife at home bit.'

'When do you start?' Cameron asked, suddenly sitting down at the table again.

'Next Monday. I have two assignments, just local. I'm working more as a freelance.'

'Fine. If that's what you want. I hope it's a success for you,' he muttered. 'Now, what did you say about pudding?'

His face was a mask. Even the clear blue eyes gave nothing away.

★ ★ ★

She lay awake beside him for most of the night. He seemed obsessed with having a family and was obviously determined to get his way about everything in this marriage.

He'd hurried her into the engagement, demanded an early wedding, and even the honeymoon had been organised to tie in with his business trip to Australia.

They did not talk again about either her job or his wish for children. The weekend was both relaxed and busy.

Cameron invited her parents over for a meal, and Jane and Ewan were also there, so it turned out to be a pleasant family occasion. With the redoubtable Mrs Baines to provide perfect meals, there was nothing for Megan to do but enjoy herself.

'Wonderful to see the two of you so happy,' Megan's father said as her parents were leaving. 'I couldn't have wished for a better son-in-law if I'd scoured the county for him myself.'

'Dad!' she exclaimed. 'I thought you had!'

'That was your mother! Always

wanting to make sure her chicks were well and truly launched before we retire, so there would be plenty of grandchildren, ready to be spoiled.'

'So,' Cameron said, after their guests had left. 'Your parents are also hoping for grandchildren. Shame that they are unaware of your feelings.'

Megan stared at him.

'I was thinking,' he went on. 'How would you like it if we reopened the stable block? We could get them done up and then buy a couple of horses.'

'Oh, Cameron, that would be wonderful. My very own horse? I always dreamed of having a pony. But you do realise what you'd be letting yourself in for? They don't come cheap, you know, and then there's feeding and vets and everything.'

'I'll look into it next week. There are bound to be some horses for sale locally. I'll contact the builders and get the stables checked over. Perhaps you'd forget this working nonsense if you had a new interest.'

'Surely you're not trying to bribe me? You're not expecting me to give up my plans for working in exchange for a horse, are you?'

He shrugged.

'I'm tired. Ready for bed. Leave the clearing up for Mrs B.'

Megan put down the dirty glasses she'd been collecting and switched the lights off. So, Cameron's generous suggestion had strings attached. Was having a baby such a big deal? Should she give in and accept her new role in life? But it was a huge, momentous change that she was not ready for. Marriage was so complicated. Was romance truly all it was cracked up to be?

Trouble And Strife

Megan's job wasn't mentioned again that weekend, and early on Monday morning, Cameron left for London.

The job that the editor of The Bucks Guardian had asked her to do was a simple assignment, a council meeting, rather mundane, but the bread and butter of small papers. He also asked her to cover a local amateur dramatic production later in the week.

'And be nice to everyone. This isn't the West End and they are amateurs. Say what you think of the play itself. It's one of the classic amateur things. That way you only offend the author. Local people always expect a decent review, whatever their performance. You'll be bringing a fresh eye to the umpteenth production by this particular group. I'll give you a couple of tickets, then the hubby can go with

176

you,' the editor said cheerfully.

Megan grimaced. Cameron would hardly relish being called 'the hubby'. Nor would he like the idea of attending some local amateur production. She could see trouble ahead, but she could hardly turn down her first assignment.

She took the tickets and smiled.

'I'll do my best. Thanks for giving me the chance.'

'I'm sure we're all glad to have you on board. I'll be asking you to cover a crafts exhibition next week. Some of our local ladies are taking their handywork to a national show up in Birmingham. It's quite an occasion for them, so we'll give it good coverage. You might need to spend the night away but, obviously, we'll pay expenses. Probably not what you're used to but this isn't London. Don't suppose the hubby will object, will he? He must be proud of his wife.'

'I'm not sure. I suppose it will be all right.'

'You'll have to be flexible, my dear.

Can't have a story breaking without a reporter to cover it. We all have to turn to and help out when needed.'

'Of course,' Megan said quickly. 'You can rely on me.'

If Cameron didn't like the thought of her working, what on earth would he say to this bit of news? An evening spent working this week and a night away next ... she could already imagine sparks flying.

* * *

He arrived home late and in a bad mood that evening after his train had been delayed. He kissed her absent-mindedly as he came in, and she sensed it would be best to keep quiet about her own plans, at least until after dinner.

She poured him a glass of wine and handed it to him in silence.

He slumped down into one of the comfortable armchairs and leaned back, his eyes closed. He looked so weary.

She was filled with a sudden surge of

love for him. He looked so vulnerable as he lay back in his chair and she began to realise how hard he had to work for his success. Perhaps she was being unfair to him. He had offered her everything she could want.

Why was it so important to make a career for herself?

She bit her lip and frowned, then crossed the room and kissed him on the top of his head. His eyes flickered.

'That was nice.' He reached out and pulled her towards him. She sat on his knee and kissed him again. He smiled at her.

'You are exactly what this man needs after a bad day. A beautiful wife, tender loving care, and a good meal.'

She smiled, then remembered that — if she kept on with her part-time job — she wouldn't always be there for him when he came home at the end of the day.

'Penny for them?' he asked, as he stared at her.

'Don't waste your money.' She

laughed. 'Shall I ask Mrs B to serve dinner or do you want to change first?'

'I think I'd rather change first, and maybe take a shower.'

She reached out a hand and heaved him from the chair.

'You'll have to hurry then.'

While she waited for him to get ready for dinner, she picked up a magazine and flicked the pages, bored, and thinking how her life had changed since their marriage.

She was left on her own for so much of the time. If they had a baby, it would keep her busy. And they could always have a nanny to look after it for some of the time, so she could maybe have children and still work.

Then, over dinner, Cameron made a suggestion. 'Jane and I have to go away later this week. There's a wine festival on in Edinburgh and we need to be there. Why don't you come, too? It might be fun. You can meet some of the people I deal with up there. What do you say?'

Megan thought quickly. Edinburgh sounded fun but she had to cover her drama assignment.

'You go on your own,' she said. 'You'll enjoy spending some time with your friends. I'm sure you don't really want me tagging along and I certainly don't need any more shopping. No, I'll enjoy a quiet day or two. I might go up to London and catch up with Lisa and all her gossip.'

He looked disappointed.

'But I'd like to have you there. In fact, I really want you with me. I want to show you off. You can see Lisa any time. You can spend a day with her next week and then we'll go on to a show.'

'She's a working journalist, Cameron. She can't just take a day off when she feels like it.'

'I want you to accompany me to Edinburgh,' he insisted. 'You complain you have nothing to do. Well, I'm giving you something. Oh, I suppose Edinburgh isn't glamorous enough for you. Well, I'm sorry. This is my life. My work. It provides all the good things you like to have around you. Money has to be earned. I'm asking you Megan. Accompany me on this trip. It's important to me.'

'Well, excuse me!' Megan was furious. 'But I was happy with much less before I met you. I only had a tiny flat, and wouldn't have dreamed of spending day after day shopping for things I don't need. Don't try to pretend it's providing for me that keeps you so busy. You have your own agenda.'

Cameron said nothing. Eventually, Megan broke the silence.

'When do you have to go?' she asked.

'Wednesday. Returning late on Saturday — or Sunday if you'd prefer it. We could stay over and see a bit of the city if you like. I promise you, it's a lovely place. You won't be bored.'

'I'm sorry but I have a job, too. I can't come with you on this trip. I may not be a high-flyer like you Cameron, but my work is important.'

Megan was standing her ground over this and was determined not to budge.

Cameron and Jane caught the late afternoon plane for Edinburgh. He'd said nothing more to Megan about her accompanying him and had packed his own suitcase, leaving her alone in the huge, empty house.

She set out early for the drama production, arriving well before the show was due to start because she wanted to chat to a few of the actors and stage crew, and maybe pick up some background information.

The group was well-known locally and was usually well-supported by their audiences.

When she entered the little hall, the stage curtains were closed and a few people were rushing around frantically. One of the programme sellers asked if she needed any help, and as soon as they knew she was the reporter from the local paper, she was given VIP treatment. The lady producer came out to speak to her and gave her a run down on the group, the show, and the difficulties of getting enough males of the right ages to cast the play.

'Anything you want to know, dear, just ask me. Anything at all. Now, if you will excuse me, I should go backstage and give my little flock a few last words of encouragement.'

The woman scurried off, leaving Megan reeling.

She was given a programme and took her seat, declining the front row that was offered, preferring to sit unobtrusively farther back where she could listen to the comments of the audience, which was always a good indication of how it was going.

By the end of the first act, Megan was beginning to feel slightly desperate. It was a very poor production, with casting that was all wrong. Her creative writing skills would be stretched to their limit if she was to give them a favourable review.

She decided to make her slant an appeal for new blood for the group, if her editor would go along with it. After all, the producer herself had made the same point. She gritted her teeth and settled down for the final act. She had to find something good to say about the wretched play.

As it moved towards its climax, she breathed a sigh of relief and applauded with the rest of the audience. Thank heavens Cameron hadn't been there.

As she drove home, she asked herself was her ambition really going to be fulfilled by such assignments? Was this job worth risking her marriage for?

She let herself into the empty house and realised this was the first time she had been completely alone for several weeks. Then she realised that she rather enjoyed the feeling.

She went through to the kitchen and put on the kettle and searched for some instant coffee.

'Comes to something when I can't even find coffee in my own kitchen,' she muttered. But, she acknowledged, it wasn't really her kitchen. It was Mrs B's.

She went to her little den and worked on her piece for The Bucks Guardian until it was late and well past bed-time.

★ ★ ★

For the next two days, Megan found she enjoyed the temporary freedom of being her own person. She gave Mrs Baines a couple of days off.

'Tell you the truth, Mrs Marshall, I shall be glad of the chance to go and see my daughter for a day or two. She's expecting, you know, and I'd be relieved to see she's keeping as well as she says. Thanks ever so much. Mr Baines will be around, should you need anything. And there's always plenty in the freezer. Now, if you're sure, then I'll get on my way.'

Megan stared round the immaculate kitchen and felt tempted to leave a few things lying about, just to mess it up and make it look homely.

On impulse, she phoned Ewan and arranged to meet him at a pub they used to visit when she lived at home.

'So, how's married life treating you?' her brother asked cheerfully as they found seats for themselves.

'Fine. It's good to see you. And how about you? Or should I say, how about you and Jane? Any news imminent?'

'Unlike my impetuous sister, we are in no hurry.'

Megan smiled and nodded. Maybe if she and Cameron had taken more time, she wouldn't be feeling quite so worried about her own future.

'Whatever do you do with yourself all day, all alone in that big house?'

'I've got a part-time job. Writing for the local rag.'

'And how does Cameron feel about that?'

'He isn't happy. Let's talk about something else. How's Dad?'

Ewan sensed that something was troubling his sister but wisely said nothing. She would confide in him if and when she was ready. Obviously all was not quite as it should have been.

Megan returned home around ten. The answerphone was flashing and she pressed the message button. Cameron's voice filled the room. He was obviously not pleased to find that she'd gone out, and had left a few curt words, hoping that she was managing. There was no message of love; no endearments. Evidently, she had not yet been forgiven for refusing to accompany him. A couple more days and he would be home again.

* * *

Megan went back into the house on Saturday morning after taking a stroll around the garden. Immediately, she saw that the answering machine was once more flashing. Somehow, each time Cameron had phoned, she hadn't been in the house and he'd had to leave a message. And whenever she tried to call him back at his hotel, he was out of his room. This was the longest time that they'd gone without speaking since they'd met.

She pushed the button to play back the message, expecting to hear his voice.

'Hello? Mrs Marshall? Mrs Baines here. Oh, dear, I hate these machines. Hope you can hear me? It's about my daughter. She's really quite poorly and if it's all right with you, I'd like to stay on for a few days more. What with her expecting and all. I'm ever so sorry. 'Bye then.'

Megan smiled at the message. Poor Mrs Baines. She'd gone away for a little holiday and ended up working, as usual. It was just as well that Cameron was away.

Megan wandered into the kitchen and poked around the fridge, looking for something for lunch. She put a piece of cheese and an apple on a plate and went out into the garden to enjoy the day. The sun was warm and she dozed in the hammock on the veranda.

She awoke to the sound of raised voices.

'She can't possibly have gone out,

leaving the house open like this. Megan? Megan where are you?'

She almost fell off the hammock with shock. Cameron was back. He had come back early and was talking to someone. She went round to the kitchen door and pushed it open to find him standing there, looking his usual immaculate self.

'Hello,' she said. 'You're back early.' She moved towards him, but he made no reciprocating gesture and continued to speak.

'There didn't seem much point staying without you. I've brought some friends back. They're here for the weekend.'

A momentary panic ensued as she remembered the absence of Mrs Baines but there was nothing she could do as Cameron brought in his guests.

'Miles and Davina, you haven't met my wife. Megan, Miles and Davina Wilson, friends from way back. They were out of the country for our wedding. Now, what would you both like to drink?'

'A cup of tea would be wonderful,' Davina replied.

'No problem. Can you organise it, Megan?' Cameron said, as he motioned his guests towards the lounge. 'I don't think you've seen the house since it was finished. I'll give you the tour.'

She stood in the kitchen, helplessly looking at the retreating figures. No Mrs Baines, and an untidy mess of paperwork in the bedroom that she'd intended to tidy away before Cameron's return.

If the Wilsons were here for the weekend, she would have to provide meals for them. Having spent the last few days snacking on anything she could find in the fridge, she had no idea what food there was in the freezer and, out of the blue, she was expected to entertain house guests. She didn't even know if there were clean sheets on the spare beds.

She gave a shrug.

If Cameron invited people without even telling her, it was his problem. She banged the kettle on to the Aga and put cups and saucers on a tray. She opened a packet of biscuits she found in the cupboard and emptied them on to a plate. No home-made goodies today. Tough.

Several minutes later, Cameron came into the kitchen. He crossed the room and put his arms round her. She lifted her face for a kiss but, instead, he looked around.

'Where's Mrs B?' he asked.

'Her daughter's ill. She's away for a few days.'

'How on earth will you cope?' he asked, suddenly looking worried.

'We shall have to manage between us, won't we?'

She peered into his face trying to read his expression.

He gave a swift grin.

'I've missed you.' He leaned over and kissed her. 'I'm sorry I was so cross,' he murmured. 'I behaved badly and I was wrong to think I could make you do something you didn't want to. Forgive me?'

'Of course. But there are things we

need to talk about. And right now, one of them is what are we going to do about dinner?'

'Surely there must be something in the freezer? Can't you organise it? Jane and, probably, Ewan as well will be back for dinner. If you're really stuck, Jane will have to rustle something up when she arrives. Now, shall I take the tea through?'

He poured the water into the teapot and carried the tray to his guests.

Megan opened the freezer and, joy of joys, found a casserole dish, carefully labelled and with a 6 ringed in red. That must mean six portions, she thought happily. Some rice with it and an ice cream pudding to follow. She could surely cope with that?

She followed Cameron into the lounge and accepted a cup of tea.

The evening passed off smoothly and as everyone made their way to bed, Megan decided she would ring a local restaurant the next day to book Sunday lunch.

Sunday passed pleasantly. Cameron had made no comment about the lunch arrangements and remained the perfect host at all times. The conversation had been light and trivial for most of the day and, despite Megan's feelings of tension and strain, she had liked the visitors well enough.

'Do you work with Cameron?' Davina had asked during lunch.

'Good heavens, no,' she'd replied. 'I'm a journalist. I don't somehow think Cameron would need my sort of skills in his business.'

'Oh, I see. I didn't realise you worked. How on earth do you manage to keep that enormous house so beautifully?' Davina continued.

'I have help, usually. She's away at present.'

Megan had caught Cameron's look of anger at the mention of her job.

'What will they think of me, if my wife has to go out to work?' he said later. 'It doesn't build much confidence in my friends or customers if you imply that you have to work.'

'Sometimes, Cameron,' she said sweetly, 'you are the most chauvinist man I have ever met.'

They sat in the kitchen sharing canned soup and bread rolls.

He said nothing about the meagre supper, although he had hated every mouthful of the synthetic-tasting soup. He was still smarting about being called a chauvinist. Maybe she had a point. He knew he needed to rebuild some bridges, though the look on her face suggested he was still saying the wrong things.

'I really love you, Megan,' he said. 'You do love me, don't you?'

'Yes, of course. I'm just a little afraid at times that your obsessions rule you too much.'

'I hope you'll get involved with my business at some time. It will help you to understand a bit more. There will be several other trade shows similar to Edinburgh before Christmas. Maybe you'll think about it.'

Megan's mind raced. She and Cameron desperately needed to talk if this marriage was going to be a happy one. She loved him and he obviously loved her but their love needed deeper foundations.

Their main problem was that they'd missed out on getting to know each other in all their haste.

★ ★ ★

Mrs Baines returned the following afternoon. She seemed full of life and had enjoyed her stay with her daughter, even though there had been a few anxious days.

'She's right as ninepence now. Just a bit tired. Now, let's see what we need to buy in. I expect we're out of everything. I'll get Mr Baines to drive me to the shops and order the rest by phone.'

Megan smiled at the kindly woman. Obviously, her presence was no longer wanted in the kitchen. She needed to find something else to do.

As if on cue, the phone rang.

'Darling? I've been given tickets for that new musical that everyone's talking about. A client has invited us to join him and his wife this evening. If you drive in, we can travel back together. You can park at that place off Tottenham Court Road, you know where I mean? I'll meet you at the theatre at seven. OK?'

'Well, I suppose so,' Megan replied.

'You don't exactly sound thrilled,' he commented.

'It's just a bit out of the blue. Fine, I'll meet you at seven. Which theatre?'

The arrangements were made and Megan went back to the kitchen to pass on the news to Mrs Baines. But she'd already left for the shops, so Megan scribbled a quick note. She went upstairs to decide what she could wear and was again interrupted by the telephone.

'Hi, Megan. This is Henderson, Bucks Guardian. I need you to cover another council meeting this evening. Reg has gone off sick and there's no-one else free. It's a very important meeting about the new shopping development. I wouldn't ask at such short notice but that's journalism for you.'

'Oh, dear,' Megan replied. 'I've arranged to go out this evening.'

'Sorry, love, but this is crucial. I did warn you that I'd call on you at short notice. Now, are you serious about working for us?'

His voice held a warning note. This was make or break time as far as the editor was concerned.

'Of course I'll do it. No worries. I'll rearrange my evening.' She crossed her fingers as she spoke, sensing an almighty row ahead.

She dialled Cameron's mobile number. Should she tell the truth or make some other excuse? This was yet another test of her resolve to keep a career.

The calm voice of the recorded message irritated Megan. Cameron must be in a meeting and had turned off his phone. She left a message explaining briefly that something had come up and that she couldn't make it to the theatre that evening. She would explain later and hoped he enjoyed the show.

$$\star \quad \star \quad \star$$

The council meeting was taken up with the usual parochial trivia that was so vital to a small community. It was hardly a major debate. Feelings were heated and the final voting was close, but the motion to pass the plans was approved. Megan glanced at her watch. For one wild moment, she contemplated driving into London to meet Cameron and his clients as they came out of the theatre. She might just make it if the traffic wasn't too heavy. The thought passed. The chances of meeting the group were too slight to make the effort worthwhile. She drove home.

There were lights blazing all over the house when she got back which was unusual because Mrs Baines was so careful about not wasting electricity.

Then she realised that Cameron's car was parked in the drive and she could see his shape through the lounge window. As she drew to a halt outside the front door, he came racing out to meet her.

'Where have you been?' he demanded. His expression was thunderous.

'I left you a message,' Megan whispered.

'What message? I've been frantic with worry. I've been phoning police all round the county in case you'd had an accident.'

'But I thought you'd be at the theatre.'

'Theatre? Did you think I could possibly sit through some show when my wife might be lying in a ditch somewhere?'

'I left you a message on your mobile. Sorry.'

Cameron grabbed his mobile and pressed the play back message button. He listened briefly and switched it off.

'Well?' Megan asked.

'Try playing your own messages back, then you'll see how I felt.'

He stomped off into the kitchen and she played back the messages.

They were all from Cameron, asking where she was with increasing degrees of anger. The final one was timed at eight-thirty, and said he was on his way home. Megan bit her lip. But what else could she have done?

In silence, she went upstairs and began to get ready for bed. Her notes on the meeting would have to wait until the morning. Equally silently, Cameron joined her in the bedroom and after showering, he got into bed. The king size bed seemed to stretch away to infinity, with the two of them lying as far apart as they could.

★　★　★

In the morning, Cameron announced that he planned to work at home for the day.

'Maybe we could have lunch out somewhere?' he suggested. 'We need to talk.'

'I suppose so,' Megan replied. She had planned to write her report that morning and then deliver it to the paper, but after last night's fiasco, there was an even more urgent need to clear the air. Breakfast had been very tense.

Cameron went into his office to work while Megan went into her own den and quickly typed up her notes from the meeting.

Then everything was changed with a phone call. It was Mona, sounding desperately worried.

'Megan? It's your father. He's been taken into hospital.'

'What's wrong with him? Is it serious?'

'We don't know yet. They're doing tests. I'm so afraid it's his heart. He's been overdoing it for months. Anyhow, I'm going to the hospital now. I'll call as soon as there's any news.'

'I'll come straight over. Where is he?'

'Milton Keynes. They thought that was best. Our local place doesn't have the facilities.'

'I'll meet you there. Is everything OK at the shops? I mean, is Ewan OK to carry on for the time being?'

When Megan put down the phone, Cameron was beside her, looking anxious.

'What is it?'

'It's Dad. He's in hospital. I must go to be with him.'

'I'll drive you. No. No arguments. I insist. I didn't have much on today, though I admit, visiting the hospital wasn't on my list of favourite things to do.'

'I'd better fax my report in. Mind if I bring it through to your machine?'

Cameron stared at her and shook his head in disbelief.

'Get your priorities sorted, of course. I'll be waiting in the car.'

Break-Up

Anxiously, Megan went into the reception area of the huge hospital, while Cameron parked the car.

She found the correct ward and looked around. She found her father in a side ward and her mother was bending over him, stroking his forehead. Megan watched them for a moment and unexpectedly, felt a slight pang of envy for the closeness they shared.

'Megan,' her mother said with some relief. 'Thank you for coming so quickly. He isn't too bad, as you can see.'

The array of wires and machinery attached to her father belied Mona's brave words.

Megan kissed both her parents and sat down.

'Been overdoing it a bit,' her father

said in a hoarse whisper.

'Poor Dad. It really is time you handed things over. Lucky that Ewan's around to help.'

It was quite apparent that her father was in some discomfort.

When Cameron arrived, Charles Belmore looked relieved.

'Cameron, my boy. Good to see you. There's a favour I need. Would you . . .'

'Be quiet, darling,' Mona urged her husband. 'I'm quite sure that Ewan can cope and Cameron can always help out if need be.'

'I'll do whatever I can. Now you stop worrying and concentrate on getting better.'

It seemed a long morning, punctuated by visits from nurses and doctors, coming to take samples and make checks.

Cameron left to see Ewan. He was relieved to have something positive to do instead of making polite conversation.

It was afternoon before the consultant arrived to see Megan and her mother.

'He's had a mild heart attack. Nothing too serious. A couple of days and he can come home. This is a warning, though. His workload must be reduced. Fortunately, he is a fit man for his age and apart from a few changes to his diet, I see no reason why he shouldn't have many years ahead of him. Provided of course, he removes the stress from his life.'

Mona wiped away a tear and clutched Megan's hand in relief.

'I couldn't manage without him. I'll make certain we follow your advice, Doctor. Thank you.'

★ ★ ★

For the next few days, Megan found herself fully occupied just driving to and from the hospital. Cameron was a tower of strength and was always on hand, ready to help and advise Ewan when needed, but Ewan was finally in command and proved that he had inherited his father's talent for business.

With all the drama, Megan's trip to Birmingham had slipped to the bottom of her list of priorities. It was just another thing she had to cope with. She had a perfectly good excuse to get out of it, with her father's illness, but she knew she might be jeopardising her future with the paper if she didn't do it.

Charles was to leave hospital on the Wednesday morning and Mona insisted that she would rather she and her husband spent a few days quietly at home alone.

So Megan realised that there was nothing to stop her from carrying out her assignment and that if she drove back late at night, she wouldn't need to stay over. Her next problem was breaking the news to Cameron.

'You're unbelievable,' he said when she told him of her plans.

'I don't see why. Mum distinctly told us they wanted to be left alone. I'll drive up to Birmingham in the morning, after you've left for work, and I'll be back during the evening. Probably before you, knowing how often you have to work late.'

Cameron held up his hands in a gesture of surrender.

'OK. Fine. You have your priorities. You know what you want. Who am I to argue?'

Megan felt the chill in the air. She had qualms about the stand she had taken but now it had reached the point of being a matter of principle.

'Cameron, could I borrow your mobile for the day so that I can keep checking that everything's OK with Mum and Dad? My phone seems to have gone on the blink.'

'Of course,' he replied. 'And I'll sort out a new phone for you tomorrow, so that you've got one for the day after.'

He handed his own mobile to her, and she slipped it into her bag before going through to the kitchen to see how dinner was coming along.

The kitchen, as always whenever Mrs Baines was cooking, was filled with wonderful aromas emanating from the oven.

The two women chatted and Megan asked the cook if she would leave something out for Cameron the following evening.

'I'm not sure how long I'll be so I'll get something on my way home,' Megan told her.

★   ★   ★

Early the next morning, Cameron left for his visit to London and Megan drove up the motorway towards Birmingham and the National Exhibition Centre. It was an easy drive and she wondered why the editor had considered it necessary for her to stay over. A few interviews and a look round and she could easily be home by early evening.

The group of women she'd been sent to interview proved to be both lively and interesting. They were excited about their craft hobbies and they were hoping they could turn them into small businesses. They sat on a pile of boxes at the back of their stand and shared sandwiches and coffee.

Megan made her notes, putting in plenty of personal details about the group, their hopes and ambitions.

'Phone me when you get back and tell me how you get on,' Megan suggested. 'I wish you the very best of luck. I think your plans are great.'

As she drove home, she thought how pleased Cameron would be that she was early, but as she pulled on to the drive she saw that the house was in darkness.

She ate some of the food that Mrs Baines had left out for him, realising that he would have eaten out by this time. Then — although she'd already phoned her several times from the exhibition — she called her mother again and promised to go over the following day. Mona told her that Jane was at the house visiting Ewan and was staying over. By this time it was almost eleven o'clock and there was still no sign of Cameron, so Megan decided to go to bed, fell asleep straightaway and woke suddenly at three o'clock to find herself still alone. She went to look in the spare rooms in case he'd decided to sleep there to avoid disturbing her. But no, she was definitely alone in the house.

Perhaps he was trying to make some obscure point. Restlessly, unable to sleep, she went into her den and began to write up her article.

She had an early breakfast and was sitting in the warm kitchen munching her toast when Jane came in and poured herself some coffee.

'Everything all right?' her sister-in-law asked conversationally.

'Cameron didn't come home last night. I was worried at first, but then I decided he must have had a late meeting or something. How did Dad seem?'

'Fine. Your mother is coping perfectly. Look, I'm sorry, I've no idea

211

where Cameron is. Try one of the warehouses. There's a list in the office. He may have arranged to see someone early this morning and stayed over.'

'Thanks. I'll leave it for a while. He may phone.'

She mooched around for some time and finally went to look for the numbers Jane had mentioned. She dialled one at random and spoke to a secretary.

'I'm sorry, Mrs Marshall, but Mr Marshall never tells us where he will be. I can give you his mobile number if that helps.'

'No. I already have that, thanks.'

If he had bought a new mobile yesterday, she would have no idea of the number and his was still in her bag.

There was little she could do, so she decided to visit her parents as planned. She left a message for Cameron with Jane and drove off.

★ ★ ★

'We've reached a decision,' Mona announced over coffee. 'We're going to move to a smaller house. A bungalow, we think.'

'Good grief!' Megan exclaimed. 'I never thought I'd see the day. Is it because Dad's health is worse than you thought?'

'Who's this you're talking about?' her father asked as he entered the room. 'If I'm not with you all the time you're talking about me behind my back.'

He sat down heavily, exhausted by the effort of moving around.

'Mum says you're looking for a smaller house. I think it's a splendid idea.'

'You're sure you wouldn't mind, Megan?' Mona asked anxiously.

'No, of course not. I won't ever want to move back here.'

There was a trace of doubt in her voice and her mother looked at her sharply.

'Everything is all right, isn't it? With you and Cameron, I mean.'

'Of course we're all right. Why wouldn't we be?'

There was absolutely no way that she could worry her parents at this time. If she needed to talk to anyone, it wouldn't be either of them.

When she returned home, there was still no sign of Cameron and she looked around anxiously for a message from him, but there was nothing. He was asserting his independence just as she had.

He eventually returned home that evening at around six-thirty.

'Hello, you. Had a good day?' he asked chattily. He seemed to be in a good mood.

'Not bad. Went to see my parents. Dad seems well, considering.' She tried to chat casually about the routine things, neither mentioning her trip to Birmingham nor asking where he had been the previous night.

He poured drinks as if nothing had happened at all.

Megan felt disturbed.

It was not that she wanted to check up on him but a whole night spent away from home, without explanation . . . but if he wasn't going to tell her, she wouldn't ask. Maybe he was trying to punish her?

★　★　★

Early the following week, Megan realised that she still hadn't done anything arranging to meet up with Lisa, and phoned her old work colleague.

'How are you? And how's that gorgeous husband of yours? When are you coming to see us?' Lisa asked excitedly.

'I wondered if I could come down tomorrow? We could go for something to eat after work. I could come into the office and say hello to everyone first. I've got a couple of ideas to run past James, if he's in a good mood.'

Over dinner that evening, she decided to tell Cameron about her plans for the following day.

'I don't know what you're doing tomorrow, but perhaps you could meet up with Lisa and I for dinner?'

'I was planning an evening at home tomorrow and I'd hoped you'd be here. I'm thinking of asking one of our clients over. I owe him hospitality but I'll have to confirm it.'

'Cameron! You've never said anything about this to me. I've made arrangements with Lisa, now. I haven't seen her for ages and I wanted to run a couple of ideas past James.'

'For heaven's sake, Megan. You know my opinions on this pointless writing. Oh, carry on scribbling away. It's obvious what's most important to you.'

Megan sat at the table seething with anger. He was impossible.

'You seem to have one set of rules for yourself and different ones for me. You can stay away overnight without even telling me where you are. I want to go out for one evening and you go mad. Well, you'll just have to entertain these guests on your own. I shall be in London.'

She left the table and went into her little den. She switched on her computer and began to type up some notes.

It was always her work that caused problems.

She worked late and went into the kitchen to make some cocoa. There was no sign of Cameron. She wandered round the kitchen, touching the knives, saucepans and dishes. Everything was the best quality and none of it hers. The tiny cupboard of a kitchen at her flat was devoid of most cooking utensils, but it was her own.

Perhaps she should visit the flat the next day. It seemed pointless to keep it but the little flat was precious to her; a memory of another life. She had been a different person then. She loved Cameron but he wasn't an easy person to live with. On the other hand, neither was she.

Deep in thought, she watched the milk boil over. She poured what remained of it into the mug with the cocoa powder, leaving the mess. It was a silly little rebellion. She perched on a stool and sipped the comforting drink. It reminded her of being a little girl when life was easy and uncomplicated.

'Oh! I thought you'd be asleep already,' she said, when she went into the bedroom.

'No such luck, I'm afraid. Did you finish your work?' Cameron asked. He was sitting up in bed, reading some reports.

His voice sounded quite normal, casual even. Their earlier disagreement seemed to have been forgotten and she relaxed.

'I was just making a few notes,' she said.

'Megan. Can I ask you something? Don't fly off the handle but I have to ask. Do you think we ought to see the doctor? I mean to say, we've been married for several months now and there's still no baby on the way.'

'It's less than four months, Cameron.

That's nothing compared to the time some people wait. Besides, I've told you, I'm in no hurry to start having a family.'

'I still wonder if we need to take some tests. Just to make certain. You may still be young but I'm getting on a bit.'

'Oh, yes. What are you? Thirty-three? Positively ancient.'

'I want to enjoy my kids and not get worn out playing ball with them.'

'I think there's plenty of time before that happens.'

She was trying to keep her voice light. She knew why she wasn't pregnant. Because she had made quite certain that she wouldn't be.

'But how can we be sure that there isn't something wrong? Really, darling, I'd be happier if we could get a check up.'

'You're making a fuss. We'll have a baby when the time is right.'

Cameron sat up suddenly.

'What are you saying?'

'I'm not saying anything, Cameron, except that you are being too anxious.'

'I'd really be happier if we both had some tests. I'll call a doctor at one of the clinics. Morning or afternoon?'

'What?'

'Which do you prefer? Morning appointment or afternoon?'

'Cameron. Listen to me. You're doing it again. Trying to push me into things. We don't need any tests.'

She had to tell him the truth.

'I've been taking the pill. I'm not pregnant because I made sure I wasn't. I want to have your baby . . . babies. But not yet. Let us have some life together first.'

'How could you, Megan? How could you?' His face went very pale. 'You know how very much I want us to have a family.'

Megan moved away from him. He looked so angry. She knew she'd been wrong to take this decision without discussing it, but it had seemed right at the time.

'Cameron, it's my body. You can't want a baby before we have fully established our own roles in our marriage. You've had problems enough in accepting that I am a person in my own right. You're angry that I want a career. But I must be allowed a say in our decisions. Especially when they affect my body.'

'Of course you have a say, but you've taken control. You didn't even try to talk about it.'

'And would you have listened?'

'I can't believe you'd do that without discussing it! I don't know you at all! I'm going to the guest room.'

* * *

She slept fitfully. Why had she been so stupid to confess to taking the pill? But he'd been insisting on seeing a specialist, so what else was she to do?

Cameron had already left for work when she went downstairs. She decided that she couldn't face travelling to

London, and phoned Lisa, making the excuse that something had come up and apologised.

It was a very long day.

At seven o'clock, she sat in their lovely lounge with a glass of wine. She glanced at the old French carriage clock on the mantelpiece. If he caught his usual train, Cameron would be home by seven-thirty.

She finished her glass of wine and poured another. Dinner was waiting in the kitchen. She had only to warm it through. It reached eight-fifteen. Then eight-thirty. Perhaps he wasn't coming home at all.

Two nights' absence in just over a week.

Maybe he too was regretting their hasty marriage and had met someone else. Tears pricked her eyes at the thought. She cursed herself for being so stubborn. Why would he stay away?

Eventually, she threw their meal into the bin and went to bed. This was the end. Her short marriage was over.

She'd have to go and stay with her parents and pretend she'd gone to help her mother to look after her father.

Whether it was her decision or the wine, Megan slept soundly.

She padded along to the guest room first thing next morning, to make certain that Cameron had not returned late and slept there. But the room was unused.

She tapped gently at Jane's door and went in.

'Cameron didn't come home last night. I don't suppose you know where he is?'

'He said something about the theatre. I assumed you were going too. I'm sure he said 'we'.'

'No. I thought he was entertaining some clients here but I must have made a mistake. Sorry to disturb you.'

Sadly, Megan went down to the kitchen and plugged in the coffee machine.

Then she went back upstairs and began to pack up some clothes. She collected her laptop and printer. Maybe this was the time to write her novel.

While the coffee was filtering through the machine, she took her luggage out to the car.

If Jane or Mrs B came in, she would have to explain where she was going, and what would they make of the situation? She neither knew nor cared.

After drinking a final cup of coffee, she left. She turned to look back at the house she had grown to love and, wiping away a tear, drove off.

It seemed like the end of so much.

'It's only things that I'm leaving behind.'

She'd worked out her story by the time she reached her parents' home. She'd also stopped crying and promised herself that she would cry no more.

'Hello, you lot! Surprise!' she called as she let herself in through the back door.

Running Away

'Megan?' her mother said peering out of the lounge. 'We're enjoying a lazy breakfast in front of the fire. Seems like winter's arrived. To what do we owe the honour of this visit so early in the morning?'

'Cameron's away and I fancied some company. I hoped you wouldn't mind. Beside, I thought it was about time I did something to help my lovely parents. Any more toast? I'm famished.'

'It's lovely to see you. Dad's looking much better, don't you think?'

'He certainly is.'

'Why do you women have to talk about me as if I'm not here?'

'He's obviously better.' Megan nodded to her mother. 'Got his grumpy temper back. Must be a good sign. Right. If you spurn my nursing skills, I'll help you to house hunt. Now there's an offer you can't refuse.'

'You're like a whirlwind, Megan. Dad is supposed to be keeping quiet.'

'You know, my dear,' Charles interrupted, 'I think a bit of life around the place may be just what I need.'

'Is it OK if I stay in my old room?' Megan asked her mother.

'Oh! Well, yes, of course. I didn't realise you were planning to stay over.'

'I can hardly do much in one day, can I? I was hoping to stay for a few days, at least.'

'You're sure everything's all right?'

'Of course. Now, which estate agents have you called?'

Every time the conversation turned either to her or Cameron, Megan skilfully moved it on to something else.

★ ★ ★

'My goodness,' Mona said happily, as she served dinner, 'this is even better than old times. Fancy me having both my children home again at the same time. It's lovely.'

Mona was so happy that Megan dreaded telling her the news. Her parents would be devastated when they learned that she had left Cameron, especially when they knew the real reasons.

Her father went to bed early and Mona went up with him, leaving the young ones to chat.

'Are you sure everything's all right with you and Cameron?' Ewan asked.

'Of course. Why wouldn't it be?' she replied carefully.

'I haven't forgotten the state you were in before the wedding.' He stared at his sister and smiled gently. 'You can talk to me, you know. I won't say anything to the parents or Jane.'

'It's nothing. Cameron's away for a few days and I felt like spending some time here. Dad is much better but his illness gave me a shock. Made me realise that even parents are vulnerable. Anyway, I've been hearing good things about you. Quite the rising tycoon aren't you?'

Ewan was content to chat about the business.

When they finally went up to bed, he gave Megan a hug as they parted on the landing.

'Just because you're older than me, it doesn't mean you have all the answers. I'm wiser than you think. Goodnight, Megs.'

'Goodnight, Ewan. You're all right, for a little brother.'

Megan lay in her old bed and felt like a child again and, somehow, safe and secure.

★ ★ ★

For a couple of days she was able to carry off her role as the dutiful, caring daughter, but at dinner that evening, her mother looked hard at her.

'You are quite exhausting, Megan. I'd forgotten what life was like with you around. You're like a hurricane blowing through the house. I don't know how Cameron puts up with you. How long did you say you were staying?'

'Do you want to get rid of me?' she asked in hurt tones.

'No, of course not. But I've got used to a quiet life.'

'I'm sorry. I'll get out of your hair tomorrow. I'll go to London and see if Lisa's got time for a good gossip. While I'm away, you can decide which you like best of the two places we looked at today and I'll take you for another look round.'

'There you go again! We can look at houses on our own, for heaven's sake.'

As she lay in bed that night, Megan sobbed herself quietly to sleep, as she had done every night since she'd moved back to her old home.

When she went into London the next day, everyone at her old office had seemed pleased to see her and James had agreed to look at some of her proposed articles. She even broached the subject of rejoining the paper but he wouldn't give her any commitments.

Lisa could only spare her a short while after work and later, after a superficial chat and a cup of coffee with her friend, Megan found herself waiting at the railway station for the train that would take her to her flat.

It was strange walking down streets that, until recently, she had known so well. She let herself in and pushed away the heap of junk mail that had piled up behind the door. Apart from the build-up of post, the flat was totally tidy and quite unlike the home she had known. There was nothing out of place in the kitchen, and the fridge was empty and clean. It didn't seem like her flat any more.

'I shall sell it,' she said aloud. 'Or maybe I could let it.'

In a more positive mood, she shut the door of her old home behind her and went to catch a train back to her parents' house.

★ ★ ★

Mona and Charles found their daughter rather more subdued than usual and worried that something was seriously wrong.

'Are you sure you're all right?' Mona asked after a couple of days. 'You've become very quiet.'

''Course I'm all right. Why wouldn't I be? Now, are we going to look at those houses again?' she asked brightly.

Mona frowned. Her daughter was not telling the whole truth.

When Ewan came home from work that evening, he suggested that he and Megan might go out for a bar snack. Their parents welcomed the idea, saying they could then look forward to a peaceful evening.

The local pub was warm and friendly with log fires roaring up the chimney and Megan relaxed, knowing she could drop her pretences for a couple of hours. It was time to talk.

'So, what's new?' Ewan said, sitting beside her and placing their drinks on the table.

'Not much. Persuading our parents to decide about their future home is nigh on impossible. They just don't seem to know what they want.'

Ewan sat quietly listening to her floods of words.

'Bottling it up doesn't help, you know, sis. Nor does all this frenetic activity.'

'What do you mean? It's got to be their decision.'

'I don't mean the parents. You know what I'm talking about. Stop rushing around for five minutes and talk to me.'

'I can't. It stops me having time to think.'

'Tell me about it. We all want to help you know.'

'And admit that everyone was right and that I am a prize idiot? Not my style.'

'Cameron is being just as stubborn.'

At the mention of his name, Megan looked up sharply.

'I suppose you and Jane have been discussing us, have you?'

'Cameron's drifting round as if he has lost his fortune. I've told you, I'm willing to listen. Jane and I are sick of our siblings and their ridiculous behaviour.'

'I'm so miserable, Ewan. I don't know what to do.'

'Talking about it would be a start.'

Megan smiled and took a deep breath and told him everything.

'So that's about it. I've backed myself into a corner and I don't know how to get out of it.'

Ewan had listened carefully, making few comments.

'I suppose you think I'm a stupid idiot to just walk out without a word.'

'I think you're right to want to hang on to your career. You're not the type to sit quietly at home. Surely a man as intelligent as Cameron must see that?'

'Evidently not. If he wanted a nice quiet little woman to sit at home and produce endless babies, he chose the wrong one. Thanks, little brother,' she said, squeezing his hand. 'I feel better for unburdening myself.'

'Just some words of advice, Megs.

Don't throw your marriage away. You and Cameron have something very special. Jane told me she's never seen him as happy as he's been since he met you. It's worth sorting things out. Running away isn't the answer.'

'You may be right. But we rushed into marriage far too soon. We never allowed ourselves time to discuss the really important things. If we'd realised our fundamental differences, we wouldn't have married in the first place. I think we should cut our losses and get divorced. I can get a proper job again. Even go abroad.'

'Wait, Megan. Don't rush into a divorce in the same way you rushed into your marriage. Give yourselves time to think. Think what you'd be missing. Neither of you is any better off living your lives apart.'

★ ★ ★

Megan spent the next couple of days working at the offices of The Bucks

Guardian. It was very much more laid back than her old paper and she felt like a fish out of water there, but it was a job.

She tried to immerse herself in the articles that she'd been asked to do, but the trivial nature of the reports did not inspire her.

The editor, Mr Henderson, was complimentary about the quality of her work but he was a shrewd man. At the end of the second day, he called her into his office.

'This isn't really what you want, is it, dear?'

She stared at him.

'I think you need something more demanding. Something you can get your teeth into. There's nothing wrong with your work but you lack passion. Odd. I rarely misjudge character. You seemed to have drive and passion when you came for your interview.'

'You'd like me to resign, I take it?' Megan asked bluntly.

'Now, I didn't say that. I suggest you

take a bit of time out and decide exactly what you want from your work. I'm thinking of you rather than the paper. Give it some thought and I'll see you next week.'

Feeling subdued, Megan left the building. This could be the last working visit she would be making to this office. She was certainly no-one's gift to journalism at the moment.

Odd how Mr Henderson had mentioned passion. Since she'd left Cameron, that was exactly how she felt. Devoid of all passion.

She sat in her car, eyes closed, and reflected. If she'd had less passion and more common sense, then she wouldn't be in this mess now.

But her whirlwind romance had burnt itself out as quickly as it had begun. She started the car and drove towards the car park exit.

Someone sounded their horn.

She glanced round and then braked.

Jane rushed over and leaned through the window.

'Megan. Lovely to see you. How about a cup of tea somewhere? I'd like a chat.'

'There's nothing to talk about,' Megan replied icily. 'I'm sorry, Jane. I have no quarrel with you but there's no point talking.'

'I'm having a meal at your parents' place this evening. I thought we might clear the air before then?'

Megan sighed, parked the car again and locked the door, wondering what on earth she was going to say to her sister-in-law.

'There's a little café just on the other side of the square. They do wonderful éclairs.'

Megan laughed. 'Well, don't eat too much. Mum will never forgive you if you can't manage to finish your dinner.' She was trying her best to sound light but it was not going to be easy.

The café was crowded and steamy.

'Looks like the Christmas rush is starting early this year,' Jane remarked as they sat down.

'Christmas?' echoed Megan. It surely couldn't be anywhere near Christmas?

'We're at the end of November.'

'I suppose so we are,' Megan said, sounding bemused.

Jane ordered tea and éclairs and leaned back in her chair.

'You look pale, Megan. How are you? Really, I mean.'

'Oh, you know,' she muttered.

The two women chatted inconsequentially, Megan avoiding any questions and Jane desperately trying not to push her into giving some answers.

'You were right, these éclairs are wonderful.' Megan crammed the last piece into her mouth, wishing she had never agreed to this meeting. 'I'd better push off now, though. Mum might want a hand with dinner.'

'Look, I know you're avoiding the subject of my brother but, I wondered, just how much has he told you about his past?'

'I know your parents died when you were both very young. He had to grow up too quickly but he seems to have made a huge success of his life. Anyhow, that's all irrelevant. If you'll excuse me, I must leave. Thanks for the tea.'

She stood up, wondering how she could get out of dinner. Facing Jane across her parents' polite dining table would prove an impossible strain.

'Did you know that you're his second wife?'

Megan sat down again abruptly.

'What?'

'Cameron was married before. Over four years ago.'

'I don't believe you. He couldn't have been married before and not told me.'

'Ask him about it.'

'What happened?'

'You'll have to ask him,' Jane said again. 'You really should meet and discuss things. Then you might understand him better. Now, I must go if I'm going to be at your parents' by seven. If you decide you want to see him, then I'll pass on the message.' She left the table.

Megan sat stunned. She obviously knew next to nothing about the man she'd married. How could he have kept silent about such a major, dramatic event in his life as another marriage?

'Can I get you anything else?' the waitress asked, coming to clear the table. 'Only we're closing soon.'

'What? No, thanks. Sorry. I'm just leaving.'

In a trance, she left the café. She could hardly believe what she'd just been told.

★　★　★

'You look dreadful, darling,' her mother said as she went into the kitchen. 'What's wrong?'

'I think I may be getting flu. Would you mind if I went straight to bed?'

'What's happening, Megan? Please tell me. Dad and I are so worried about you.'

'I'm all right, really. I'm a bit run down, that's all. It's a cold or something. I don't want to pass anything on to Dad so it would be best if I had an early night.'

'What a shame. Jane's coming over this evening. You'll miss her.'

'Sorry. I'll have a bath and go to bed. Is there any soup?'

'Of course, darling. I'll bring some up later.' Mona frowned. There was something dreadfully wrong with her daughter and she wished desperately that they could talk.

After a comforting bath, Megan lay on her bed, staring at the ceiling.

She had to admit to an all-consuming curiosity. She wanted to know all about Cameron's mysterious first wife. Questions burned in her brain. Why had they split up? Where was she now?

A knock at the door brought her back to the present. It was Ewan.

'Mum wants to know how you're feeling.'

'I'm OK. Not good company though. But I wouldn't mind some soup?'

'I'll bring it up. Jane says hello by the

way.' He stared at his sister. 'You look wrecked. What's up?'

'Oh, you know. I expect Jane's told you everything. I think I may also have been sacked from my part-time job. I have to get some passion in my life by next week or that's it.'

'You're not making much sense.'

'Soup, Ewan? Spare me the lectures. I have to work out my problems for myself.'

* * *

She spent the next day in bed, her anxious mother frequently popping in with cups of tea and coffee. Megan claimed she had a severe headache, which wasn't entirely untrue.

'Just leave me to sleep, Mum,' she begged. 'I'll be fine.'

'The doctor is due to see Dad tomorrow. I could ask him to see you as well.'

But Megan shook her head. No doctor could possibly sort out this mess.

She was left alone for several hours.

Which was just what she needed — time and space to herself.

Maybe she should go back to her London flat for a few days, but the idea did not appeal one bit.

In the end, she simply stayed in bed for a couple of days and turned her problems over and over in her head until she was dizzy.

But, after two days of soul searching, she was ready to see her husband and talk. She was ready to face Cameron.

★　★　★

The lovely old house stood in the winter sunshine, looking warm and inviting. Her heart was pounding and she steeled herself for what lay ahead.

She considered knocking but decided against it; after all, this was supposed to be her home, too. So she let herself in at the front door, and walked through the hallway, gazing around as if she were seeing it for the first time.

She pushed open the lounge door.

The room was empty. The fire was laid, ready for someone to put a match to it, but the air felt chilled, as if the room had lain unused for several months. The dining room was also empty. She braced herself and tapped on the kitchen door, expecting Mrs Baines to be there, busily cooking. But that room, also, was tidy and bore no signs of activity.

She went through to Cameron's office and knocked at the door. There was no answer. Peering in she saw that his computer and his fax were hidden under their dust covers. Perhaps he'd gone away.

She went upstairs to their bedroom and opened her wardrobe. All her clothes hung in neat rows, sweaters folded on their shelves.

Then she peered into Cameron's wardrobe, put out a hand, took hold of one of his sweaters and buried her face in it. Tears burned her eyes but she fought them back. If she left this house forever, what was she going to miss? The truth hit her at every turn. The only thing she'd miss would be Cameron.

She went back down to the kitchen, wondering what to do. Perhaps Mrs Baines had a day off and would be coming in to cook dinner later. She went into the lounge and lit the fire that was laid ready. She was determined that she would wait for him. It might be a long day but that would not deter her.

She realised now that Cameron Marshall was worth fighting for.

★ ★ ★

She spent the afternoon wandering round the house, returning every so often to the lounge to put more fuel on the fire. She had sat in this room so many times during the course of her short marriage, waiting for her husband to return home from work, that it felt like one of those old times.

How would he feel when he found

her waiting for him?

But it was already nine o'clock. Perhaps neither Cameron nor Jane was coming home at all that night.

Eventually, sadly, she damped down the fire and prepared to leave the house.

In less than an hour, she could be back in midst of her warm, loving family.

She shut the door. Her attempt at reconciliation had fallen flat and it was all her own fault for not checking that he would be there.

★ ★ ★

'Megan!' her mother shouted as soon as she arrived back home. 'We've been so worried about you. Where on earth have you been? Oh, I can't believe your timing. It's too bad.'

'What do you mean?' she asked.

'Cameron. That's what I mean. I'm surprised you didn't pass him on your way home. He only left a few minutes

246

ago. He's been here all afternoon and evening. He wouldn't say what was going on but it didn't take much to work out that you've left him. You are a wicked girl to try to hide it from us. We both knew there was something badly wrong. We would always stand by you, you know that.'

She paused for breath and Megan ran to her. They hugged each other, both of them in tears. Then Megan pushed her mother away.

'What did he want?' she whispered.

'He wanted to talk. He wanted to know if you were ever going back home with him. I'm not asking you to tell me anything you don't want to, but we're here for you, whatever you decide. Look, if it's any comfort to you, we'll forget about moving. You'll always have a home here if you need it.'

'Thank you, Mum. I'm sorry for causing you so much trouble, but I've been at Cameron's house all afternoon and evening, waiting for *him* to come home. I thought it was time we talked.

Ironic, isn't it? He was waiting here; I was waiting there.'

How could they have come so close and missed each other?

Devastating News

'Have you decided what to do about Cameron?' asked Megan's mother at breakfast the next day.

'I've thought about nothing else all night, and I don't know whether to call him or not. I'm fairly certain that he came here looking for me because he wants a divorce.'

'You're not serious?'

'Oh, I'm serious, all right! Do you know that he stayed out for two whole nights the other week and never said a word about where he'd been. No explanation, no apology, nothing. And neither did he feel the need to tell me that he's been married before. It doesn't sound like a marriage built on trust and honesty, does it?'

Mona's face was a picture. She could hardly believe what she was hearing.

'I'm sure he wants a divorce,' Megan

went on. 'But I'm not going to sit back and watch while he takes the initiative. I'm not going to make things easy for him. If he wants a divorce, he'll have to fight for it in the courts.'

★ ★ ★

'Come on, sis. Let's go for something to eat at the pub for a change,' suggested Ewan that evening. 'Little brother insists. No excuses. It'll do you good to get out and it would give Mum and Dad a break from us.'

Megan didn't want to go out but hadn't the energy to argue.

And so they drove to a pub a couple of villages away, and Megan chose something from the menu, hardly noticing what it was. While her brother went to the bar to give their order, she sat with her back to the room, staring moodily into the fire.

'Hello, Megan,' said a voice from behind her.

She swung round.

'Cameron. What are you doing here? No, don't tell me.' Megan's heart began to pound. 'I've been set up, haven't I?'

Behind him, Jane and Ewan were standing, looking pleased with themselves.

Ewan spoke first. 'Don't be cross, Megan. We had to do something. We couldn't stand by and watch while the two of you destroyed yourselves. Jane agrees with me. This nonsense has gone on quite long enough. We're going to leave you to talk, but we'll be close by if you need referees,' he joked.

'You scheming . . . ' she hissed at her brother and then turned to Cameron. 'Are you leaving or shall I?'

'It seems a shame to waste their good intentions. And you do want to talk. You came to see me yesterday at the same time that I tried to see you.'

'How did you know?'

'The fire had been lit. A trace of your perfume? I've missed you, Megan.'

She faltered. His eyes looked soft and strangely vulnerable. Cameron never looked vulnerable . . . it wasn't in his character.

She cleared her throat. 'There are things you must explain if we are going to be honest with each other.' She hoped she sounded positive and that he couldn't see how much she was trembling inside.

'You want to ask me some questions? Fire away,' Cameron offered.

'Why didn't you tell me you'd been married before?'

His jaw dropped. 'Who told you that?' He glanced across at his sister and his eyes narrowed. 'It was Jane, I suppose.'

'Yes. She mentioned the fact the other day, assuming that I already knew and was very surprised that you had failed to share that little detail with me.'

'Megan. It was all in the past. I've nothing to hide.'

Her food arrived, and she stared at the steaming plate and felt slightly sick.

Cameron picked up her fork and put it into her hand.

'Come on, or your brother will thump me for ruining your appetite.'

She paddled the fork through the food, hoping that if it was moved around, it would look as though she had eaten something.

'Where were you those nights you didn't come home?' she asked him.

'In a hotel. You made such an issue about being independent that I thought I'd clear out of the way and leave you on your own to see how you liked it. It was a petulant reaction but I was hurt.'

'Jane said you were at the theatre one of the nights you didn't come home.'

'I took one of the secretaries as a treat for her. I'd already missed one performance of that play the night you'd cried off at the last minute, and when my clients got more tickets I couldn't refuse them. I didn't ask you to come with me because I knew you were busy. See? I was just trying to give you the independence you insist that you crave.'

'But Cameron, by independence I

mean that I want is to be able to go out to work, not for you to leave me on my own. I enjoy being with you.'

'But you don't need to work. I want you to be around to share my life. I give you a generous allowance and you have only to say if it isn't enough.'

'You still don't understand do you? I do need to work. And when you didn't come home, I was worried half to death.'

'But you didn't even ask where I'd been. So I assumed you didn't care. That's why I stayed out again a few nights later.'

His wife stared at him. He sounded plausible, but then, didn't he always?

'That food looks jolly good. Do make an effort to eat something, darling,' he told her, a look of concern on his face.

Megan stirred the food around again and made an effort to put some into her mouth. It tasted like sawdust.

'You still haven't told me about this previous marriage of yours.'

'There's nothing to tell. It was over a

long, long time before I met you.'

'Is she still around? Do you see her?'

Cameron went white with anger. Then he stood up and glared down at her.

'I told you that it was over long ago. You don't listen. You seem unable to understand real, deep feelings. You're more interested in your precious job than caring for me. I'm sorry I interrupted your climb up the career ladder.'

Now it was Megan's turn to go white. She stood up in an attempt to put herself on more equal terms with him.

'You're quite unbelievable, Cameron. Someone fails to follow your exact plan and you manage to transfer all the blame. You're no better yourself. Caring is understanding how a person thinks and accepting their needs as well as your own. No wonder your first marriage didn't last.'

'I think it's time to stop this,' Ewan said, crossing the room to stand beside the pair.

'This is all your fault,' said Megan,

turning towards her brother. 'Now, if you don't mind, I'd like to go home. Cameron and I have nothing more to say to each other.'

'Easy, Megs. Give it one more try? You haven't eaten your food,' he ended lamely.

'There's only one thing this food is fit for.'

To everyone's horror, she picked up her scarcely touched meal and upended the plate all over Cameron.

She giggled hysterically as she watched the soggy mess drip down from his immaculate shirt and on to his jeans.

Everyone in the room was watching and Ewan and Jane stood open-mouthed, neither of them quite knowing what to do next.

Suddenly amazingly calm, Megan picked up her bag and walked to the door. 'I'll wait in the car for you, Ewan,' she said quietly, although she was shaking inside, partly with anger and frustration and partly in shock at what she had done.

Ewan murmured an apology to the landlord while Cameron stood speechless. Never had anything like this happened to him before. Jane began to scrape the food back on to a plate and, apologetically, she asked one of the bar staff for something to clear it up.

'Don't worry, love. I'll see to it,' the landlord offered, stifling his laughter. 'Do you want something to wipe the stains off your clothes?' he said, turning to Cameron.

'Give me a napkin to get the worst off. It could have been worse. I might have been wearing a good suit.'

'Good luck, sir,' the landlord said as Jane and Cameron left.

As soon as they had walked out of the door, a hubbub of talk and laughter broke out behind them.

Cameron was furious. He didn't like being made a fool of.

Megan would pay dearly for this. Maybe he had totally misjudged her. Could it be that she'd married him only for his money? Well, if she thought she was going to divorce him and get a handsome settlement, she had another think coming. He would get the finest legal advice and she would not get a penny more than he could help.

★ ★ ★

'Are you all right, sis?' Ewan asked anxiously as they drove home.

'Never better,' she assured him. She felt furious with herself for losing her temper like that but boy, had it made her feel better!

'Look, I'm sorry that Jane and I interfered. But our intentions were good. It seemed that you needed to talk.'

'I don't really blame you, Ewan. Unfortunately, that pompous, self-important creep simply doesn't want to understand my point of view. No, I think I'm well out of it.'

'Oh, well. He's a wealthy man. You should do all right out of the divorce.'

'What!' she exclaimed. 'Ewan. Stop

the car this minute.'

Ewan obeyed.

'Whatever's the matter?' he asked. 'Do you feel sick?'

'I'm sick of people. You surely don't think I'd touch a penny of his money? I'd go busking in the underground rather than take a penny from him.'

Megan would not have anyone suggesting she had married Cameron for his money. No way.

'Well, don't be too hasty. After all, you gave up a good job because he didn't want you to work after you were married. You deserve some sort of financial compensation.'

'But I don't want anything from him.' She giggled. 'Did you see the look on his face? It was worth making an exhibition of myself, just for that.'

'I must say, I was pretty shocked myself.'

'Somewhere deep in our past, an ancient ancestor must have had the foul temper that goes with the red hair.' Megan was sounding much more in control of herself.

'Ready to face the parents?' he asked.

'Ready as I'll ever be. Don't suppose they'll be too thrilled at the news.'

'You're not wrong. They had high hopes for tonight.'

'You mean they knew? Ewan, that wasn't fair. Dad's not supposed to be stressed.'

'It was Mum's idea in the first place. If you want, I'll go in and tell them things didn't work out. That way you can go straight to your room.'

In the darkness, Megan nodded. She felt unbelievably tired and accepted his offer gratefully.

* * *

When she awoke the next morning, Megan felt as if her head would burst. She felt sick and heavy. Her mother knocked on her door and came in with a cup of tea.

'Are you all right? I was so worried about you.'

'I suppose Ewan told you all the sordid details about what happened last night,' she said bitterly.

'All Ewan said was that it hadn't worked out. What sordid details, Megan? What on earth happened?'

Megan recounted the events of the previous evening.

Mona laughed out loud.

'Sounds like he got what he deserved. But I'm afraid you may have ruined your chances of any reconciliation. Cameron is too proud a man to accept that sort of treatment. Now, drink your tea and I'll get some breakfast for you.'

'I'm sorry, Mum. I really don't feel well. Do you mind if I stay in bed for a while? I don't want anything to eat or drink.'

'What's wrong with you? I expect it's just the tension.'

'My head aches. And I'll have to make an appointment to see Dad's solicitor later on. I'm afraid there's no future left for this marriage.'

'Oh, Megan. I'm sorry. I knew you

261

should have waited.'

'Spare me the *I told you so's*. I'm just sad I couldn't have had a marriage like yours and Dad's. You've always been so happy together.'

'Yes, but it took some working at, I can tell you. There have been many times when it wasn't all plain sailing.'

Megan stared at her mother in surprise. She'd always seemed content with her life, so patient and always there, waiting at home for them all.

'Did you ever want to do anything for yourself? Have a career?'

'Oh, yes. I once had great plans to become a concert pianist.'

Megan's jaw dropped. Her own mother, a concert performer? Never.

'So why didn't you?'

'I'd never have been good enough. Anyhow, I met your father and all my foolish ambitions went out of the window. It saved me a lot of heartache from trying to achieve the impossible.'

'I didn't even know you could play. We haven't even got a piano.'

'I sold it. When you were on the way, we needed so many things and there was no money to spare. Dad was establishing his first shop and was so full of plans. I knew I'd never have time to keep up with my music so it seemed sensible to sell the piano to buy all the baby trappings you'd need.

'I never really missed it once you and Ewan arrived. But there were times when your father nearly drove me potty. He never appreciated just how much work there was with small children. He wanted his dinner parties, just the same as ever and, always, the business came first. But he only wanted to provide the best for all of us. Not that this helps your situation.'

Megan sighed heavily.

'It all goes to prove how selfish I've been, worrying you and Dad so much. I'm sorry. I've been so wound up in my own affairs, and probably have been all my life, that I didn't think of the effect I was having on everyone else. I promise, I'll get out of your way as soon as I can.'

'Don't be silly, darling. We're here for you and always will be. But divorce. Is that really the only way out?'

'It seems that way at the moment.'

Megan turned and buried her face in her pillow. She still felt sick and her headache was getting worse. Perhaps if she got up and moved around, she would feel better. And she needed to make an appointment with the solicitor. What a hopeless mess she had made of her life; of everything.

Mona went out of the room. She felt sad and angry for her daughter and couldn't bear to see her so unhappy. Clearly, the idea of a smaller place somewhere would have to wait. Did children ever really grow up? Did they ever finally leave home?

★ ★ ★

After a couple of days spent mooching around doing very little, Megan was given a good talking to by her mother.

'Right, young lady. It's time you made up your mind about what you are going to do. If you insist on going ahead with this divorce, then you need to see Mr Bryce. But if you want to have one more go at trying to get back with Cameron, then now is the time to see him and discuss the options.'

Mona was unusually forceful. She needed to know what the future held for all of them.

'You are right, as always,' Megan agreed. 'I'll phone Mr Bryce and make an appointment.'

'And how are you feeling now? You really do look awful. Your eyes are dull and your hair has lost all its condition.'

'My nose is dry and I'm a poor sick dog,' Megan tried to joke. 'It's stress. What's Mr Bryce's phone number?'

'It's in the red book by the phone.'

Megan made the call immediately, but as she replaced the receiver she said to her mother disappointedly, 'He can't see me until next Friday morning.'

'Right. Well, in the meantime, why

not go to see the doctor? He might be able to give you something to relax you. A tonic maybe?'

'I'm all right, really, Mum. Don't fuss.'

Mona gave a shrug. She knew better than to argue with her daughter but it didn't stop her from worrying.

Megan frowned. Maybe her mother was right. Perhaps the doctor might be able to prescribe something to help. She hated feeling unwell at the best of times and this was certainly not one of the best. She made an appointment and, saying nothing to her mother, drove off to the surgery later that morning.

★ ★ ★

The doctor dropped a bombshell. 'It looks to me as if you might be pregnant,' he informed her. 'Everything you've said leads me to think that's the cause of the nausea. I'll do a test anyway, to confirm it one way or the other.'

Megan sat stunned. Pregnant? She couldn't be pregnant. It was impossible. She had taken precautions.

She waited with a sense of total disbelief for the results of the test.

When the doctor called her back into the surgery he was beaming broadly.

'Congratulations, Megan. Pink!' He held out the tiny strip that was sealing her fate. 'It's positive. You must be very pleased. I'm sure your parents will be delighted at the prospect of their first grandchild.'

The family doctor, who had known her since she was a small child, grinned with delight.

'Now, you're a bit on the thin side. We need to build you up a bit. I suggest a course of vitamins and one or two sensible additions to your diet. I'm delighted you came back here to see me.'

'You are certain, are you doctor? I mean, there couldn't be any doubt?'

'None at all. Why do you ask?'

'I've been taking the pill.'

'Probably started it a bit too late. My guess is you were already pregnant. We'll organise a scan.'

'Doctor. The last thing I can cope with at this moment is a baby.'

'I can understand it's something of a shock, but you'll soon get used to the idea. I'm sure that husband of yours will be thrilled.'

Megan's doctor had been a guest at the wedding as an old family friend.

He didn't seem to have heard a single word she'd said.

* * *

Half an hour later she sat on a hill overlooking a wooded valley not far from her parents' home. The irony of her situation hit her hard. She had effectively ruined her marriage because her husband had wanted children before she was ready for the responsibility. Now she was pregnant anyway. What was she to do? She decided to keep her pregnancy secret for a little while, at least until she had time to decide what to do for the best. She still had to keep her appointment with the solicitor, although it all seemed futile now. She even regretted her impulsive gesture at the pub the other night. If nothing else, that had blown any chance of getting back with Cameron.

It was well into the afternoon before she returned home, and she realised that she had missed lunch, again thinking only of herself. A trifle sheepishly, she went into the house and through to the kitchen. There was a covered plate with a slice of homemade quiche and some salad that had been left for her. It looked delicious and she realised she was starving. She ate the food hungrily and washed up the plate. Then she went through to the lounge but it was deserted. Her parents were out somewhere.

She remembered she was due to go to meet her editor, the next day. He had given her an ultimatum. He had said she had lost her passion. How right he was. She knew that it was pointless trying to defend herself and that she would be unable to work at all soon, anyway, so she might as well resign. It was the only sensible thing to do. Once Cameron learned of this latest development, he would know he had truly won.

★ ★ ★

When Megan returned from her appointment with the editor of The Bucks Guardian, she felt subdued. She had burned her boats. She no longer had a job, nor any income, however small. And, although she'd told Ewan that she wouldn't accept a settlement from Cameron, that had been before she knew about the pregnancy. Now everything had changed.

Still, the thought of actually having a baby was quite terrifying. Apart from carrying it around for months on end, and giving birth, it would be up to her to provide everything for it. Feed it when it needed feeding; change nappies; understand what it wanted when it cried. And how could she ever work again? What a nightmare it all was.

She heard her parents coming in, and soon they were all sitting together in the kitchen, sipping tea as they talked.

'We've been to look at another bungalow,' her mother told her. 'It's absolutely lovely. Only a couple of miles away. It's just what we've been looking for and very reasonably priced. There's no hurry of course, as we said. And we could stay here, if you decided you want to live with us.'

'I don't know what to do yet but, in any case, it's much more important for you to be settled. You've considered us all your lives. I still have the flat. If I don't move back there, I might sell it and buy something else. I think it's great that you've found somewhere you like. You should go for it.'

'We haven't quite decided yet, but we are quite keen.' Mona was holding back her enthusiasm, Megan could see. She continued, 'Oh, I'm sorry. I never asked how you got on at the paper?'

'I've resigned. It wasn't really what I wanted. The editor and I both realised it. I'm not sure what I shall do next.'

'Bad business all this,' grunted her father as he flopped down in his chair. 'I'm worn out. Sort yourself out soon, my girl. Your mother's worried to death about you.'

Megan bit her lip. She was not used to hearing this sort of comment from her father, who was usually such a patient, kindly man. Obviously, she had been too caught up in her own troubles to realise just how much everyone else was suffering on her account.

'I'm sorry. I won't be a nuisance to you for much longer, I promise. Why don't you both go and sit by the fire. I could cook dinner for us all.'

'Lord preserve me from your cooking,' Charles grumbled. 'You just don't take after your mother in any way at all.'

Megan said nothing. Her father was

right. She was useless at cooking. And how much use was her writing talent, when it came to looking after a home and family?

Family! What a loaded word that was. Her mind went back to its all absorbing task of finding a solution to her current predicament.

★ ★ ★

After dinner, Ewan offered to take her for a drink.

'No nasty little set-ups this time? Promise?' she asked before she would agree.

'Promise. Just you and me. We'll even go to our own local and not the scene of the flying pies.' He grinned.

'Watch it, you.' She couldn't help smiling.

'That's better. First flicker of amusement I've seen for days.'

The pub was quiet. They'd put up some Christmas decorations and were obviously trying to liven up the trade for the coming festive season. Megan felt even more miserable at the thought of Christmas.

'Wine?' Ewan asked as they sat down.

'I'll have an orange juice, I think. For some reason I feel really thirsty.'

He fetched drinks for them both and handed her the orange.

'What's the latest with you?' he asked conversationally.

'I'm now officially out of work.'

'I see. So what do you plan to do with yourself?'

'Haven't a clue. I might start my novel.'

'You? Write a novel? You have to be joking. Besides, what will you live on while you're writing it? And while you find some mug to publish it?'

'Thanks for the vote of confidence,' she said grimly.

'You're serious aren't you?' said Ewan, startled to realise this.

Megan stared into the fire. She had a series of hazy notions for a novel that she'd always been certain could be woven into some sort of story. But now that she was being challenged, she knew they were really nothing more than a series of random thoughts that had no logical plan.

'Oh, I don't know. It's early days.'

'You ready for another drink? Something stronger this time?'

'I'll stick with the orange juice.'

'You're not pregnant are you?'

Megan's eyes lowered.

'Pregnant? Me? Don't be daft. Can you imagine me with a baby?'

Ewan sat down again, staring at his sister.

'My goodness, you are, aren't you? Oh, Megs. I have to say it, your timing is somewhat less than perfect.'

'I haven't said I am pregnant,' she protested.

'How long? I mean, when's it due? Does Cameron know?'

'I only found out yesterday.'

'I'll get us another drink,' Ewan announced feebly. 'And as you are off alcohol, you can drive us home. I need something stronger.'

'If you dare breathe a word of this to anyone, I'll . . . I'll . . . ' She paused while she tried to think of a suitable punishment. 'Especially not to Jane. I'd never forgive you. I mean it. Never.'

They talked solidly for the next hour. For Megan, it was a great relief to be able to talk honestly. She poured out all her thoughts. She knew, really, that she could trust Ewan to keep her confidences.

At the end of her outpourings, he took her hand and smiled.

'I don't agree with what you are saying, but I'll stand by you. Please do consider Cameron, though. You do still love him, whatever you say. It's quite obvious to everyone. Why don't you agree to meet him again? Preferably somewhere they don't serve food or drink.'

'I doubt he'd agree to it. But whatever happens, I'm not getting back together with him just because of the baby. I can think of nothing worse than a marriage where the children are supposed to bring the couple together.'

'If I arrange it, will you at least see him?'

'Perhaps,' she began doubtfully. 'But I can't imagine ever wanting to give up work entirely. I'll probably want to find something to do after the baby's born, so he'd have to agree to be more flexible about my career.'

Megan felt herself weakening, knowing she was about to give in to her brother's persuasion.

'Why are you doing this?' she asked, suddenly curious. 'What's your motivation?'

'I love my stupid sister. I can't bear to see you so unhappy and I also know it's worrying the parents.'

Hesitantly she agreed that he could arrange a meeting with Cameron. But she swore him to secrecy about the baby.

While she waited to hear what Cameron would say to Ewan's suggestion, Megan lived on tenterhooks, tense and snappy with everyone.

Then, the day before her solicitor's appointment, her world turned completely upside-down. A large brown envelope arrived from Cameron's own solicitor. She felt sick. Mona was most concerned.

'Whatever is it?' she asked.

'He's beaten me to it. Cameron is suing me for a divorce. What do I do now?' she wailed.

'You'd better call Mr Bryce right away and tell him what's happened. Then at least he will be prepared for tomorrow. Do you want me to come with you?'

'Thanks, but this is something I have to do by myself.'

Truce

The Belmores' kindly family solicitor was an old friend who'd known Megan since she'd been a child.

He frowned at the sight of her.

'I'm so sorry, my dear. This is taking its toll on you. Are you certain there is no chance of reconciliation?'

'No,' Megan said miserably. 'I was trying to arrange another meeting with him but I've heard nothing.'

She handed over the packet of divorce papers.

Mr Bryce read rapidly through them.

'Irrational and intolerable behaviour, eh? Sounds dramatic. What's that all about?'

Megan blushed slightly. She told him her version of the problems leading to the present situation, even confessing to the incident in the pub.

'So, how could he possibly want to

see me again?' she concluded.

The solicitor stifled a grin.

'At least you can't claim to have had a boring existence together. You'd better leave this with me and I will advise whether a simple defence or a cross petition is best. We could attempt mediation, when someone will work with you both to try and explore the options for reconciliation.'

He glanced at the papers and pursed his mouth.

'You may be better to go for the defence option. You could claim that your behaviour is not at question and that the marriage is not irretrievable.'

'But it is,' she wailed miserably.

'Leave it with me. I'll read through the papers in detail and give you a call on Monday. Cameron's a wealthy man, so you shouldn't be left destitute.'

'I don't want his money.'

'But you do have to think of the future. You shouldn't give up all your entitlements, you know.'

As she left Mr Bryce's office, Megan

thought over his words. She would always want the best for her baby, and her own pride must never ruin her child's life.

But asking for a settlement for the child meant she had to admit to the pregnancy. What a difference it would make to Cameron if he knew she was pregnant, and there was no way she could allow the baby to be the reason for him wanting her back.

She made her way through the town centre, heading for the car park where she'd left her car.

Everywhere there were Christmas decorations and lights. It was December, the shops were filling with crowds of shoppers, and this promised to be the very worst Christmas for Megan.

Then she noticed Ewan's car parked outside one of her father's shops and went in.

'Time for a coffee?' she asked. She wasn't ready to go home just yet.

'I'm a bit pushed, but if you insist. So, how did it go?'

He listened to what she said and then gave a small smile.

'I've go some news for you. I've had difficulty getting hold of Cameron because he's been away on business. But now he's back at home and is willing to talk things through with you over the weekend. He wants you to go to his place . . . your place . . . however you think of it. What do you say?'

'Go over there? I'm not sure. It's hardly neutral territory.'

'It's up to you. Those are his terms.'

Megan sat in the little office, sipping her coffee. She thought of seeing her husband again. It was almost too painful and she felt herself growing weak. How very much she loved him. She had to force herself to remember the reasons for her departure. All her principles. Just how trivial it sounded now. How little any of it mattered.

'OK,' she whispered to her brother. 'I'll go to see him tomorrow.'

★ ★ ★

Megan hardly slept a wink that night. She got up early, feeling the familiar nausea that she was desperately trying to hide from her parents. Fortunately, she had her own en-suite bathroom.

This wretched morning sickness must end soon. She had told her mother and father that she was going to see Cameron and felt slightly guilty about the look of hope that flickered across both their faces.

'You look very pale, dear,' her mother said at breakfast. 'Are you sure you'll be all right? Would you like one of us to drive you over? I'm sure Ewan wouldn't mind.'

'Ewan's busy today. And this is something that I have to do for myself.'

After trying to eat some toast, she went to her room and dressed carefully, wanting to impress Cameron with her apparent self-sufficiency. She wore a long, wool skirt and a blouse in shades of dark green that were reflected in the colour of her eyes, colours that she knew were flattering to her. She needed all the help she could muster for this meeting. She brushed her hair in an attempt to make it shine. But it still looked lacklustre.

'And pregnancy is supposed to make you bloom,' she said with a sigh to her reflection.

She put on a little make-up, hoping that her pallor would be less obvious.

'You look lovely,' said Mona as her daughter came to say goodbye.

'Wish me luck,' Megan said lightly.

'I'm not sure if luck is quite the right word. But we wish you all the best. Let us know if you decide to stay over anywhere. We shall be worrying about you.'

Megan kissed both her parents, feeling as if she was off to a job interview instead of visiting her soon to be ex-husband.

* * *

It was a damp, dull morning, and rain was threatening. Most un-Christmassy, she thought as she turned her car into the drive of her former home. There were lights on in several rooms, despite it being mid-morning.

Cameron opened the door himself. He was wearing a light-blue shirt and denim jeans. His eyes looked bluer than ever and his hair even darker than she remembered.

'Hi. Come in. I've got some coffee brewing. Go into the lounge and I'll bring it through.'

He moved easily through the large hall, clearly at ease. He was on his own territory and it gave him a definite advantage. This meeting was probably going to be another ghastly mistake.

She went into the beautiful room that she had loved since the first moment she'd set eyes on it. Jane's hand had been at work with festive decorations. A few early cards were strung on silver ribbons, with space left for the many more they obviously expected to receive. A large tree stood in one corner, hung with blue and peach baubles and shiny bows that reflected the colours of the room. Dozens of tiny, silvery lights twinkled amongst the branches and the unmistakable scent of pine filled the air, evoking childhood memories of Christmases past.

Megan and Ewan's trees had never been elegant affairs like this, so tastefully arranged. They'd always had a competition to see which of them could hang most things on each branch. The tree had disappeared under the mass of tinsel and baubles and tatty little homemade decorations, but their childhood Christmas trees had been symbols of love and sharing.

'Lovely tree,' she said almost shyly, as Cameron came into the room.

'Jane decorated it, of course. She always enjoys the festive season. You've never seen this place at Christmas. I was forgetting.'

'I didn't even know of your existence last Christmas.'

He stared at her as if realising this for the first time himself.

'Your coffee.' He handed her the

fragile china cup, the coffee black, as she always used to drink it.

She didn't like to ask for milk, a habit she had recently developed.

'Well, now, we have a lot to discuss.'

They both sat on the edges of their seats as if sitting back in a relaxed way might in some way concede a point to the other.

He looked tense. He had lines at the corners of his eyes. Perhaps he wasn't the tough, unrelenting businessman after all.

'Sorry,' they both began together. They laughed nervously. 'After you,' they again said together.

He took the initiative.

'I'm sorry that I was away when you tried to get in touch.'

'That's not your fault. But I'd have preferred to speak to you before I received your package from the solicitor.'

'I gather you have consulted a solicitor, too?' he said, showing no emotion.

'It seemed sensible. Actually, he would be furious to know about this meeting. I gather that opposing sides should only contact each other through their legal representatives.'

'Is that what we are? Opposing sides?'

'That seems the way you want it.'

'Let's try to be constructive and stop sniping at each other. There have been faults on both sides. We might begin by each of us admitting this. What do you say?'

Megan felt the blood draining from her face as she felt a surge of anger. She was not prepared to concede anything. He had been totally unreasonable throughout, refusing to see that she could even have an opinion.

'I'm not sure that we can make that assumption. I don't consider my actions were out of order.'

Despite himself and the tension that raged inside him, he laughed.

'Megan, I do understand your feelings, but now you seem to have given up trying to understand mine. It was a shock to you to discover that I'd been married before. It was wrong of me to keep that from you. But it was also wrong of Jane to tell you about it behind my back.'

'Good thing she did. It makes me feel less of a failure, knowing that you had one broken marriage already.'

'Ouch!' he said. 'One below the belt to you.'

Megan picked up her bag from the floor beside her chair.

'We are obviously hell bent on hurting each other, Cameron. Maybe we should let our legal chaps fight it out.'

'Sit down. I'm going to tell you the whole story about my first marriage and you are going to listen. When you have heard all about it, you can decide how much of a failure I am when it comes to matrimony.'

'Very well, but you needn't shout.'

She settled back in her chair, and prepared to listen, trying to look relaxed.

Cameron cleared his throat nervously and began to tell his story.

'At university, I took a business course and I became interested in wine because the father of a friend of mine owned several small vineyards in the Rhone Valley. My friend's family invited me over one summer and, fascinated by the art of vintnery, I decided to set up a wine importing business. I travelled around and established plenty of contacts.

'As you know, I was due a substantial amount of capital from my parents' insurance policy, which became available after I'd finished my education. Fortunately, I found myself in the right place at the right time. My business was successful and, as wine drinking grew in popularity, I expanded. I bought this place at a good price, with the idea of renovating it. It was a complete wreck when I found it — I know that you've heard a lot of this before but I want you to understand everything.

'When I bought the house, the local press made a big thing about it. Because I was young, it made the local headlines. Someone who worked for a film company happened to see the article and asked to come for a look round. They were looking for a film location. The film was basically a ghost story set in an old mansion, and this house was exactly what they wanted. The money was very tempting and I agreed to let them use the place.

'When the filming started, one of the stars was Sophie Stevens. You may have heard of her?'

Megan hadn't. She shook her head, and Cameron continued.

'Sophie was a rising star. She was very beautiful and, in my innocence, she seemed like a goddess. Can you imagine how I felt when she actually seemed to like me? A few weeks later, she said she had fallen head over heels for me. I was totally infatuated by her and, never believing she would agree, I asked her to marry me.

'When she said yes, I could hardly believe my luck. We were married several months later, by which time Jane had joined the firm and the wine business was growing at a fantastic rate. Jane worked from home, pretty much as she does now and, while Sophie and I went on a long honeymoon, she ran everything as smoothly as I could wish.

'Sophie and I travelled the world and everyone who knew her welcomed us both like minor royalty. I began to get a taste for luxury. Rich and famous people invited us to stay. During this crazy time, and maybe foolishly, I took huge gambles with the business and expanded like mad. I had to prove something to Sophie.

'Although my career was taking off and there was money enough for us to do whatever we wanted, my actress wife never quite managed to land the parts she was expecting — not that her confidence ever seemed dented.

'Eventually, tired of flitting from

place to place on an extended holiday, I suggested to Sophie that we should come back here and settle down. She laughed at the idea and said she would never settle in some forgotten hole in the depths of the country.

'She wanted to stay in expensive apartments in capital cities all over the world. I did, at that time, have a flat in London, but she wanted a bigger place, saying it was too small for her to have the right sort of parties. She claimed that she had to be seen all the time, if she was to be successful.

'I'd already realised that she wasn't much of an actress, and as soon as her so-called friends and movie business contacts realised this as well, and cottoned on to the fact that she was never going to hit the big time, they quickly began to disappear from her life, one by one.

'After we'd been married for only a few months, I discovered she was having an affair with a film producer. I thought I loved her enough to forgive her, but then she dropped a huge bombshell by telling me that there was no way she would ever have children. They would ruin her figure, ruin her career.

'Eventually, she left me for another movie producer who'd told her he was going to make her as famous as she thought she ought to be.

'Sadly for Sophie, not only was her career beyond salvation — she was just such a bad actress — but it turned out that the producer was already married and when his wife heard about her rival, Sophie was soon sent packing. She now lives in Croydon with her second husband, a stockbroker, and isn't very happy with the way her life has turned out. Or so I've been told. As you can imagine, we don't keep in in touch.'

'I hope this explains why I was so worried about your obsession with your career. Or, at least, what seemed to me to be an obsession. Megan, I'm sorry if my own obsession seems to be with having a family, but I want to have kids before I'm too old to enjoy playing with them. My own father was always too busy — I never remember him playing with me, and I was sent away to boarding school, so I never saw much of either of my parents. At the time that they were killed, my life seemed like one long term at school.'

★   ★   ★

His eyes were sad as he finished recounted his painful memories.

Megan sat silently, waiting until he pulled himself together.

'Would you like some more coffee?' he asked at last, willing her to break the tension.

'No, I don't think so. Thank you for telling me all this, Cameron. It does explain why you've behaved in the way that you have. But you really should have told me all this before now.' She spoke in a voice that was scarcely more than a whisper. So much had been made clear, but she couldn't quite forgive him for placing her in the same mould as his first wife.

'I'll need some time to think over what you have said.'

She suddenly realised that all the time she'd been listening to her husband's long speech, she'd been thinking about the baby.

Now she wondered who the baby might look like.

Cameron was the most handsome man she had ever met. His child would surely be especially gorgeous. She hugged the thought of her baby close to herself, sensing that she had almost reached her decision.

Seeing her husband again had been enough for her to know just how very much she still loved him.

'Will you have some lunch?' he invited. 'Mrs Baines left some soup to heat up and there's cheese and biscuits.'

She considered. It would probably be sensible for her to leave now, while they were still on reasonable terms. She needed time to think, but it was tempting to stay and hear more about this complex man.

'OK. If you're sure it's no trouble,' she said.

He went into the kitchen and she stood looking through the window. It was raining steadily now and looked most depressing.

'Do you want a tray brought through, or will we eat in the kitchen?' he asked.

'Kitchen. It's easier.'

'Come on through, then.'

★　★　★

Megan followed him, feeling as if she were a total stranger to the house.

The kitchen was warm and cosy and as immaculate as always. The scrubbed pine table was set with mats and soup bowls, and a large wooden cheeseboard filled with a variety of her favourite cheeses was placed in the middle. The fruit bowl was filled to the brim, as she remembered it usually was. Shyly, as if

297

she was a visitor, she sat at the table while her husband poured soup into her bowl.

'There,' he said, 'that should warm you up. You look as if you need something to perk you up a bit. Perhaps you'd like a glass of wine?'

She shook her head. 'Not when I'm driving,' she murmured, hoping it would be a sufficient excuse. She ate the delicious soup, savouring the rich warmth.

'You haven't shown much of a reaction to my story,' he said after several moments of uncomfortable silence.

'Well, of course, I understand more. But it doesn't really alter the facts, does it? I've become a substitute for Sophie. You're following the same course of actions. You didn't learn much from the dreadful events of your first marriage.'

'Maybe you're right. But, believe me, I really did fall in love with you the moment we met. You were so full of life and so bright. I wanted to grab you and keep you all to myself. I was so terrified of losing you. I wanted to stop you from doing all the things that Sophie had done. I'm so sorry, Megan.'

'So am I, Cameron. I wanted it to work, very much.'

'Is there really nothing I can do to persuade you to come back?'

'I'm not sure. I'm very confused at the moment.'

'But I love you, Megan,' he said simply, getting up to remove the empty soup bowls. He set a plate in front of her and passed the cheeseboard.

She loved him too, but dared not say so.

'I'm asking you, even begging you, to think about it, Megan. I love you more than I could ever have believed possible. What I felt for Sophie was nothing compared to what I feel for you. She's in my past and she's only relevant because she influenced how I treated you. I never told you about her because I wanted to forget about my past mistakes, and what had happened before didn't seem relevant to us. Now, since you left, everything I do is empty and pointless. Megan, please come back to me.'

He reached over to take her hand.

'Cameron . . . I need time. I daren't allow myself to be wrong again.'

He walked round the table and put his hands on her shoulders and turned her to face him. Tenderly, gently, he held out his hands and pulled her to her feet. He was gentle as he kissed her. She began to kiss him back, allowing his arms to surround her and pull her close to him.

'Oh, Megan, Megan,' he whispered.

'Cameron, please stop. I can't deny that I love you. You know I do. Please, let's both take time to think things through.'

'How long do you need? Any chance you can decide before Christmas? Then we can share it together.'

'I don't know. I'll call you. What about your solicitor?'

'I'll put a hold on everything until I

hear from you. Give me a chance.'

As she walked towards the door, she was certain that they could have a future together but, this time, she was determined not to rush into anything.

'Megan. There's one more thing. I hope this will convince you that I really do understand how you feel. If it means you'll come back, I will forget about having children. It would be a great disappointment, but faced with that or living without you, there's no contest. I'm certain we can love each other enough to make up for it.'

She stared at him, wondering if he could really, truly mean what he had said. His expression was serious, and as sincere as she could ever believe anyone to be. She smiled at him.

'I'm sorry about throwing that plate of food at you. It was unforgivable.'

'You're not kidding me.' He smiled. 'It was quite a shock. Mrs B could hardly get over that I'd put some washing in the machine myself. She misses you, by the way.'

'Oh, yes? I assumed she thought I was a totally useless housekeeper and wife. I'd better go now. I have a lot to think about and so do you.'

'Please don't take too long.'

A New Beginning

Although it was only four o'clock when she arrived home, it was almost dark. Her mother rushed to greet her.

'How did it go?'

'Fine, it went fine,' said Megan. 'But I need more time to think over what he said. I'm not going to rush into anything this time.'

'That's wonderful! We're so relieved.'

'Hang on, Mum. It isn't quite that clear. As I said, I'm going to think it over. If he really means what he says, then everything might be all right. He's told me things about his past that explain a lot. Though I understand why he said nothing about his first wife, he should have come clean from the start. Growing up is quite painful, isn't it? Whatever age you decide to try it.'

'Welcome to adulthood,' Mona said, with a gentle smile. She hugged her daughter. 'I'm glad you're feeling better.'

'Thanks, Mum.'

'I suppose you won't know what you are doing for Christmas, yet? No, of course you don't. I'll go and put the kettle on.'

Christmas, Megan thought. What *would* she be doing by then?

★ ★ ★

A few days later, she made a phone call.

'I wondered if you were free for dinner this evening?' she asked. 'There are few things I'd like to discuss with you.'

'I see,' replied her husband. He was trying his best to sound casual and cheerful. 'I'll look in my diary. Does this mean you have an answer for me? The answer I want?'

'Wait and see,' Megan replied.

They arranged to meet at a small restaurant about halfway between his house and that of her parents.

Once more, she dressed carefully trying to look the best she could. The nausea was passing a little and she was generally feeling better.

When she arrived at the restaurant, Cameron was already there, and she felt a thrill of delight as he stood up, holding out a chair for her. She noticed a bottle of white Burgundy, uncorked and chilling in an ice bucket. Two glasses stood beside it. She felt a slight qualm. She couldn't spend an evening drinking wine and he would be suspicious if she drank nothing but orange juice. Ah well, a small glass of wine, especially white, was acceptable, even in her condition. She smiled to herself at the news she could soon be breaking to him . . . if all went according to plan.

'It's good to see you,' he said politely, leaning towards her and kissing her cheek. 'You look lovely.'

He seemed strangely hesitant, as if he didn't know quite how to behave towards her.

They ordered their meal and continued the polite, small talk for a while.

'How long do we have to go on like this?' he demanded suddenly. 'I can't bear it. Have you reached your decision? Are you coming home to me?'

'I think so. Yes, I think so, Cameron. But this time, there have to be some ground rules.'

Whatever she had been about to say, was lost. Cameron leapt out of his seat and rushed round to her side of the table. He pulled her into his arms and kissed her.

'Thank heavens, my darling. Oh, how I love you.'

'Everyone's staring! And you haven't heard my list of rules, yet. You may change your mind when you hear what I have to say.'

He sat down again and, with an expression of simulated concentration, he propped his head on his hands, ready to listen.

She took a deep breath and began to speak.

'Rule one: I am me, Megan, not just your wife . . . not some sort of trophy to be placed on a pedestal. Rule two: if I have a job to do, you accept that it is important to me and also accept that it might take me away from home from time to time.'

'OK, so far,' he said. 'Did you realise that I have become totally useless without you?'

'Rule three: if and when we decide to have children, you will not spoil them half to death in an attempt to give them all the things you never had.'

'Did you also know you have the makings of an extremely bossy woman?' He suddenly sat up straight. 'Hey, does that mean that you will consider having babies?'

A grin spread across his face as she nodded.

She wasn't quite ready yet to reveal her final trump card. She felt confident that he did really want her for herself but she needed to be certain.

There was no way she was going back

to him just for the baby's sake, and he had been so scared that he'd lost her, that he'd agreed with everything she'd said, so far. But the final proof would lie in his future actions.

And to take the risk of putting him to that ultimate test, she had to rely on his promise that everything was going to be different from now on. As it was, she knew that everything was bound to change when she broke her final piece of news.

'Why don't we leave your car here and drive home in mine,' he suggested. 'I can't bear to be parted from you again.'

'No, I'll drive myself.'

★ ★ ★

The journey seemed to take forever and, all the way, Megan was grinning delightedly to herself, wondering exactly which moment she would choose to break her news.

He would be thrilled, she just knew it.

Her new plan was to work from home as a freelance. Modern technology made it just as easy as working in a busy office and she should be able to on working right up to the actual birth. In fact, she mused, that would make a good series. *'How I adapted my career to cope with my baby.'*

Would her mind ever stop writing headlines?

Cameron turned into the drive of their home and she followed him, parking in her usual place.

'Megan, Megan, my own dear wife. Welcome home. You know,' he said, his voice husky with emotion, 'I realise that having children isn't everything, and now, with you, I have learned that one person can be enough. You are my life, Megan. From now on, I shall always be satisfied with you. Don't leave me again, promise?'

'I won't leave you but there may be times when I have to be apart from you.'

'Of course. You are your own person.

I realise that now. I will never try to organise you in future.'

'Now, that I find impossible to believe.'

'Well, maybe only when I have to. But, seriously, darling, if you do ever feel that you want children, I shall be pleased. But I promise it won't become some silly obsession. I'm over that now.'

★ ★ ★

They awoke early next day. 'Coffee?' he asked her, as she opened her eyes and stretched.

'Don't you have a train to catch?' she asked him.

'If you think I'm going to leave my wife so soon after we've got back together, then you're mistaken. I'll go and make coffee and then we'll make plans. We ought to do some Christmas shopping.'

He looked like an excited child, Megan thought fondly as he leapt out of bed.

'I'd better call my parents. They might be panicking if Mum goes into my room and sees my bed empty.'

Mona was delighted to hear Megan's news. 'I'm so pleased for you,' she said happily. 'We'll see you both later, perhaps. I take it that it's now all right to say yes to that bungalow?'

The two chatted on for some time, until Cameron returned to the bedroom, carrying a large tray of breakfast.

'Say, hello, to your mum from me,' he instructed before Megan rang off.

'That looks good,' she said enthusiastically when she saw the contents of the tray. Mrs Baines had insisted on a full breakfast when she'd heard that Megan was back.

There were scrambled eggs, orange juice, coffee and toast. Even a dish of her favourite apricot jam. She ate hungrily, while Cameron stared at her in amazement.

'I told Mrs B not to bother with much as you don't usually eat breakfast.

Seems she was right and I was wrong.'

'I need the energy. Besides . . . ' she began. She knew the moment of truth had arrived. 'Besides, I need to eat a healthier diet. I have someone else to consider now.'

She looked up at him and smiled broadly.

'I'm pregnant, Cameron. You're going to get your wish after all.'

His expression did not change. He continued to stare at her.

'Well, say something. I thought you'd be pleased.'

'Is this why you came back?'

'Of course not,' she said, her body suddenly tensing. She hadn't even given a thought this possibility, that he would see her return as selfishly motivated. 'I wanted to be sure that you wanted me for myself.' Her voice dropped to a whisper. 'I thought you'd be so pleased.'

'It takes some getting used to. I thought you'd taken precautions?'

'I wasn't quite as clever as I thought.

You are pleased though, aren't you?'

'I suppose so, but I still have this nagging doubt in my mind. I mean, would you have come back to me if you weren't pregnant?'

'Of course I would!'

'And how long have you known? I mean, when did you find out? And when's it due?'

He still looked troubled. This was not at all the reaction she had expected.

'I found out a couple of weeks ago. The baby's due sometime around June.'

He looked punch drunk. Totally confused. 'Megan, of course I'm delighted about the baby. But you must admit, I'm justified in being slightly cynical. You've accused me of not listening. Well, you have been very insistent about your needs but we need to establish a two-way thing. I may have been guilty of being obsessive about children at times but . . .'

'Cameron, what is the problem? Come on. Black and white. Stop trying to skirt round your real point.'

'I'm horribly afraid that you only came back because it was the easiest option. Being a one-parent family would be difficult for either of us.'

'You mean you would want the child, to bring up on your own, if I hadn't come back?'

'Yes, if I'd known about it. Would you have told me, if the divorce had gone through?'

Megan blushed a fiery red. She looked away from his accusing eyes. He got up and walked across to the window and looked out, while she sat very still. The silence between them seemed to last a lifetime. Neither of them wanted to speak first. At last, he turned to her.

'If we are to continue our marriage, we must make some more ground rules, as you call them.' He held up his hand to silence her as she drew breath to protest. 'No, you'll hear me out. There are some things you've done behind my back, like taking the pill for one. And getting a job. It suggests that you're quite capable of doing what you want without considering me. I understand why but we do need to establish some sort of trust between us.'

'I'm ashamed of myself,' Megan said, her voice scarcely audible.

She'd always thought herself so up-front but, in fact, now it had been pointed out to her, she realised that she'd been as selfish as Cameron.

'If we are to bring this child up to be a decent human being,' he went on, 'then we both need to change. I have to know that you are coming back because you need *me*, not just my financial support.'

Megan was still reeling from the shock of his reaction. She'd been so concerned about making sure he didn't want her back simply for the sake of the child, that she hadn't even considered that he might have similar reservations about her motives.

'I'm truly sorry, Cameron. I'd been saving my news to tell you as a surprise as soon as I was sure you wanted me for myself and not just as someone to provide babies. I thought everything would be wonderful. I love you, Cameron, and I'm sure I always will.'

Then they were in each other's arms. But they still had some way to go before their problems were completely resolved.

They spent an uneasy morning together, both being carefully polite to each other and saying little. Both afraid to say the wrong thing, just as they were beginning to iron out their differences.

Even when Mrs Baines had welcomed Megan home, it had been in a stiff and formal manner as if she did not approve of anyone upsetting her beloved boss.

* * *

Megan was just beginning to wonder if anything could ever get itself properly sorted out when, during the afternoon, a car pulled up outside and Jane, Ewan and her parents climbed out.

'Cameron. We've got visitors. Our families. What do we say to them?'

He crossed to stand behind her, resting his hand on her shoulder.

She turned to face him.

'Was there ever any real doubt that we were meant to be together?' he whispered softly. 'There may still be some issues, but I can't live without you, Megan. I just need to be sure that I am going to be enough for you.'

'How can you even doubt it, Cameron? You are everything I could ever have dreamed of in a husband. We may have a few more things to settle but for now, let's go and see what this deputation is all about. Ready?'

They opened the heavy oak door and greeted their guests.

'Hope you don't mind the intrusion. We won't stay long,' Mona began. 'But we so wanted to see you. Everything seems to be happening at once.'

They all trooped into the lounge and Cameron did his best to make them feel at home. Jane disappeared from the room and came back a few minutes later with a tray of glasses and a bottle of champagne. Megan felt herself grow warm with embarrassment. Obviously, they had all come to celebrate the fact that she and Cameron were back together again, but it was rather premature. They weren't ready to celebrate publicly.

Jane poured the champagne and handed the glasses round.

'We wanted to be together to celebrate this occasion,' Charles began.

Megan drew her breath as if to stop his speech, then realised it would be best if she and Cameron just went along with their families' wishes.

Her father continued, 'We have a number of things to celebrate today. First of all, I am pleased to say that Mona and I have had our offer accepted on the bungalow that she had set her heart on. And then — tell me Cameron, is it a family trait to do everything in such a hurry?' He smiled at his son-in-law, who raised his

318

eyebrows questioningly. 'And then, no sooner had we told Ewan about our intended move, than he and Jane told us their news. Do you want to announce it, Ewan? Though I'm sure an announcement isn't really necessary.'

'Jane and I are getting married,' said Ewan, grinning from ear to ear. 'She has done me the honour of accepting my proposal.'

'Hang on a minute.' interrupted Jane, 'Aren't you going to get down on one knee and do it properly, in front of everyone?'

They all laughed and toasted the happy couple, while Jane showed off her glittering sapphire and diamond ring.

'Isn't it just gorgeous?' she exclaimed.

'I'd like to propose another toast, if I may,' Charles went on, holding up his hand for silence. 'To Cameron and Megan. May their lives together move on happily, from this time forward.'

'To the future,' everyone agreed.

'Shall we go the whole hog and give

them the rest of our news?' Cameron whispered to Megan.

She gave a slow, uncertain smile. Then she nodded.

The expression on Mona's face — when Cameron asked her what was the secret of bringing up a happy family, and would she share it because he and Megan were shortly to have a family of their own — was one of sheer incredulity. She took a large gulp from her glass before she spoke.

'And since when have you known about this?' she demanded. 'Funny. I always thought I'd know the moment you were pregnant, Megan, but I never even guessed at it.'

'Yes, I'm only just getting used to the idea myself,' said her son-in-law, so fully in control of himself that Megan suddenly knew everything was going to be all right.

'Well done, sis,' Ewan muttered in her ear. She smiled and squeezed his hand.

'And the same to you, little brother.

Thanks for all your support. It looks like this is going to be quite a Christmas, after all.'

* * *

Christmas Eve morning was overcast, dull and dreary. 'Much too warm for snow.' Megan sighed as she looked out at the lifeless garden.

'Sorry we can't oblige with the full Christmas snow scene,' Cameron said, getting out of bed and going over to stand beside her, his arm round her shoulders. There was a new tenderness between them. Lately, they had spent hours talking, and sharing their inner-most thoughts.

'Come on. We have an important day ahead of us. Now, I've an early Christmas present for you somewhere here. Hang on.'

He groped under the bed and then handed her a large, wrapped box.

'Can't I save it till tomorrow?'

They were going over to her parents

for Christmas Day, and for Megan, opening presents together was a most important ceremony.

Mrs Baines would be spending Christmas Day with her own family, and so Mona had insisted on cooking what would be their last family Christmas dinner at their old home.

But before then, later today, everyone would be coming over to Cameron and Megan's for a special Christmas Eve meal.

'Nope. This present is to be opened right away this morning. As I said, we've got an important day ahead of us. Now, come on. Open it up.'

She pulled the ribbon off the box and lifted the lid. Inside was a cream wool dress, soft and with a long, full skirt. She held it against herself and twirled round.

'It's gorgeous, darling. Thank you. I gather it's for wearing at dinner tonight?'

'No. I want you to put it on straightaway. We have a date this morning.'

But he wouldn't say any more about his mysterious plans.

Once dressed in her new attire, she went downstairs to discover she'd been banished from the kitchen completely, and wasn't even allowed to know what Mrs Baines was planning for the family dinner.

Nor was she allowed access to the dining room, to help lay the table.

In the lounge, she fiddled with the decorations and looked at the cards until, finally, Cameron wrapped a cream, fine woollen shawl around her shoulders.

Like an excited child expecting a treat, she bounced out to the car, where he gave her a spray of creamy white orchids to pin to her dress as they set off.

'Cameron, just what are you up to?'

'You'll see in a few minutes.'

★　★　★

After circling around a couple of neighbouring villages, he turned back towards home and pulled up outside their own village church.

'What was all that about?' she demanded, 'and why are we here?'

With an expression of total bewilderment, she got out of the car. It was too early for any of the Christmas services and she couldn't think why else they would be at the church at that time of day.

'I thought it might be nice to remind ourselves of our wedding vows,' Cameron said softly. 'After all the traumas, it seemed like a good idea before we embark on the next great step of parenthood. I love you, Megan. Now, if you are ready?'

Then she noticed her parents' car parked nearby, and also Ewan's.

When they entered the church, she gasped with delight.

Her closest family and their dearest friends who had played a part in their wedding were waiting there for them — Lisa, who had been her bridesmaid and Gavin, who had been Cameron's best man.

'What a lovely idea, thank you, darling,' she whispered as they walked down the aisle, surrounded by smiles.

The service was lovely. Short and simple, but relevant to the occasion and very moving and, afterwards, everyone went back to the house, where Mrs Baines had a sumptuous buffet prepared and waiting for them.

'So that's why you wouldn't let me into either the kitchen or the dining-room. What a surprise!'

'I can't ever remember having a proper family Christmas before,' Jane said. 'I'm really looking forward to it this year, aren't you, Cameron?'

Her brother grinned.

'I reckon you and I have a lot to learn about family life, don't you, Jane? And how very lucky we are to be a part of this particular family.'

Mona wiped away a tear, knowing that this was the end of an era, but that new beginnings lay ahead for them all.

We do hope that you have enjoyed reading this large print book.

Did you know that all of our titles are available for purchase?

We publish a wide range of high quality large print books including:
Romances, Mysteries, Classics
General Fiction
Non Fiction and Westerns

Special interest titles available in large print are:
The Little Oxford Dictionary
Music Book, Song Book
Hymn Book, Service Book

Also available from us courtesy of Oxford University Press:
Young Readers' Dictionary
(large print edition)
Young Readers' Thesaurus
(large print edition)

For further information or a free brochure, please contact us at:
Ulverscroft Large Print Books Ltd.,
The Green, Bradgate Road, Anstey,
Leicester, LE7 7FU, England.
Tel: (00 44) **0116 236 4325**
Fax: (00 44) **0116 234 0205**

Other titles in the
Linford Romance Library:

NOR ALL YOUR TEARS

Isobel Stewart

When Christine Lawrence panics after losing her small daughter, she runs out onto the street and is knocked over by a car ... In hospital, Christine's husband Adam has something shocking to tell her: ten years ago she walked out on Adam and their daughter, and they had never seen her since! The accident had caused severe amnesia — but who is the man she keeps dreaming of now ... and perhaps loves?

MOST WANTED

Joan Reeves

Someone's been stealing designer wedding gowns and Sergeant Andie Luft stakes out San Antonio's most expensive bridal boutique. She disguises herself as a would-be bride, but the culprit escapes when Detective Bruce Benton arrives on the scene. And when he tries to arrest her, she handcuffs him and has no intention of letting him go. Bruce's fellow officers will never let him live this down, but the brawny detective really doesn't care. The lady's in charge . . . and Benton's in love . . .